pup for sale

HEATHER HAMILTON

ISBN 978-1-913276-00-3 (paperback)

ISBN 978-1-913276-01-0 (ebook)

Editing by Kat Harvey, Athena Copy.

Formatting by Gavin Hamilton.

Cover design by BesopkeBookCovers.com

For more information about the author and future releases please visit heatherhamilton.uk

For Chewie, who is priceless.

One

Monday.

Gemma hadn't planned on kicking anyone today. She actually felt measured and focused and calm. The pub was quite empty. A table of locals and a table of tourists were chatting quietly at the back, away from the bar. Their chatter mingled pleasantly with the muted sound system that played tracks from twenty years ago to make everyone feel younger than they were. She sat at a table in a shadowy corner near the bar, reading and occasionally sipping a pint of lager. The barman collected glasses, and as he cleared the table next to hers, they exchanged the briefest of nods. The gentle clinking was cosy and familiar. It was cool in here compared to the heat out on the street. The sun had brought out the slightest sprinkling of freckles on her arms, giving some colour to her pale skin. She wore a baseball cap, and although the sun streamed in the windows, it didn't reach into her corner.

Her pint was half gone when the door swung open, banging against the wall and making her glance up from her book. A drunken man stomped in and made his way to the bar. He was wearing a shiny suit and beige loafers. Just as she returned her eyes to her book the man thumped the flat of his hand on the bar and shouted, 'Service!' She glanced up again.

The barman emerged from the back of the room, his hands filled with glasses. Carefully placing them behind the bar, he looked serenely at the man, and said, 'What can I get you?'

'Jesus! You could do with a fucking haircut!' said the man. His tie lay somewhat askew, leaving the buttons on his salmon pink shirt revealed. He surveyed the pub, looking for endorsement, but the smattering of patrons had fallen quiet, allowing the tinny music to dominate in a way that it was never meant to. He didn't notice her in the corner, in the shadows, all in black. Finding no support, he returned his attention to the bartender, and with a loud exhale, said, 'Whisky, single malt.'

The drink was poured, and payment was given after a lot of grumbling about Edinburgh prices. The man's face was red, but it was hard to tell if it was from the drink, the mid-afternoon sunshine or from his general angry disposition. He struggled onto a barstool then sat slumped, sipping his whisky and checking his phone. The level of chatter rose cautiously once more. She made eye contact with the barman who gave her a resigned shrug. She held his gaze for a moment then lowered her eyes and continued to read.

The table of locals got up to leave. As they passed her, she noticed they had a female greyhound with them who stopped to sniff in her direction. She tickled the dog's chin and was rewarded with a gentle lick of the hand. She exchanged a brief smile with the owners, and they continued towards the door. A sudden commotion broke out when the drunk at the bar kicked out at the dog. He missed, but the mild-mannered greyhound took fright, her tail falling between her legs. She looked to her companions for reassurance and her slim body trembled.

'Filthy animals!' the drunk at the bar shouted. 'Shouldn't be allowed inside!' The locals exchanged looks and silently decided it was better to leave than to take on the man in the salmon shirt. They hurried out the door.

'Yeah, fuck off!' said the man. His profanity echoed to the back of the pub, providing the cue for the tourists to leave as well. They scuttled past the man at the bar, giving him a wide berth. She sat in the corner, still measured, still focused, still calm.

Finishing her pint, she straightened her back and marked her place in the book with a beer mat. Rising, she placed the book in her small rucksack, took out her purse and approached the bar. The charity tin for a local animal shelter sat on the bar next to the drunk. She knew the place well. The collecting tin had an appealing picture of a dog and a cat on it, and she dropped a few coins in. He looked at her with bloodshot eyes but said nothing. The barman was cleaning glasses with one eye on his two patrons. She replaced the purse and zipped up the rucksack, but before she could swing the bag onto her back, the man grabbed it. She spun round and stared at him.

'Give that back,' she said. The barman visibly tensed. The drunk ignored her demand and proceeded to unzip her bag, saying, 'What do we have in here?' He stood up, perhaps intending to intimidate her, but he was maybe only three inches taller than she was. He groped in her bag. The barman looked at her and then at the drunk.

3

'Give it back. Now.' Her nostrils flared.

The barman knew that look. He observed helplessly from behind the bar. 'Don't ...' he said, but it was too late.

The drunk was now laughing at her. 'Or what?' he said, oblivious to the danger.

She looked at the man, staring at him with such confidence that the sneer slid from his face. Visually measuring the distance between them, she took a steady step forwards onto her left leg and, in one swift motion, kicked him in the chin with her right leg. He fell backwards so hard that his head hit the floor, knocking him out. Her bag lay nearby, dropped onto the sticky floor. The only item that had fallen out was her book. She tutted as she picked it up. The bar mat lay by the unconscious man's beige loafers. She retrieved it, placed it on the bar and put her book back in her bag, zipping it up securely.

'Bastard made me lose my place,' she said to the barman. She felt the man's neck just under his jawline with two fingers and nodded reassuringly at the barman who gave her a pained smile. She sighed and walked towards the door.

'Bye Jimmy,' she said.

'Bye Gemma,' whispered the barman.

Two

She shouldn't have done that. Okay, she had only knocked him out, but still. It had been an overreaction, and in her world, that couldn't be allowed to happen. She stomped across the cobbles. Well, nobody there could identify her, except for Jimmy, and she knew he could be trusted. He asked puzzlingly few questions, always just got on with his job. The city was full of quiet wee bars that you could wander into at this time on a weekday to find only the bar staff for company. That was how they'd got to know each other. Well, they didn't really know each other, they would just chat, about bands mostly. Any time it got even close to personal, she would lead the conversation in a different direction, and Jimmy seemed happy to go along with that. If there was anyone else in the bar, she would just sit, reading her book, and all they'd exchange were nods. He was an unusually calm person, and on more than one occasion, Gemma had thought he might be someone who could prove useful. But it was safer for everyone if she kept her circle tight. Plus, he always seemed very peaceful, and she didn't want one of the few normal people she knew to be dragged into her exploits. As far as Jimmy knew, she was just another woman in this city who had time to hang out in pubs at odd hours of the day, and there was nothing unusual about that.

She had spotted him at a gig once. He had been near the front, and she was on the balcony, looking out onto the crowd below, trailing someone. Sometimes, she longed for a friend, someone who could just be hers. Jimmy was the opposite of attractive, but that made her like him more. Some women may have gone for the bearded, checked-shirt look, but not her. There was no possibility of complications with him. He was safe.

She pulled her baseball cap down so that it sat more firmly on her head. It was an automatic action. The weather in the windy city may be calm today, but it always paid to keep a cap securely on one's head to beat those strong gusts ... and to remain hidden. Down the Mound she walked, sure-footed and with definite purpose, along busy Princes Street and down towards Leith. Her dark attire seemed somewhat out of place among the florals and vibrant colours worn by passers-by. She normally liked to blend in, but summer clothes had a way of being distinctive and easily recalled. Her current attire was unmemorable and would fit in when she ended up somewhere shadowy, which she inevitably would. Dark clothes had a practical element to them that she liked. There was no place for a white T-shirt where she was going.

It felt good to have a purpose. Years ago, she had walked these streets without one. It had been lonely and dangerous. Still, she'd learned a few things. More than a few things. She'd learned not to trust people. She'd learned self-reliance. She'd learned the ways of criminals and how to be one. The lost feeling from those years was behind her now but knowing how to defend herself was a skill that was never going to be wasted. Edinburgh was very peaceful, but like any city, it had its villains, and Gemma could normally spot them a mile off.

Leith Walk was a street that represented the diversity of the city. Creaky old pubs sat alongside trendy new ones. Flats sat above bustling Thai, Italian, Indian, Ethiopian, Mexican and Chinese restaurants. Sari shops gave way to computer repair shops and shoe dying services. There were long-established record shops and brand-new coffee shops, and the price of beer varied wildly from one bar to the next. People in office wear brushed their expensive blazers past men in shabby tracksuits and baseball caps, while large, lumbering smokers were dodged by pony-tailed joggers. All this bustle meant people didn't notice what was really going on, not unless it was specifically part of their lives. If you were running for the bus or on your way to get cash out for the betting shop, why would you notice anything or anyone else in this busy place? The main hub of any shady operation was surely out in the countryside, in a massive, unremarkable-looking shed. It wouldn't be hiding here, not in plain sight.

She found the property she'd been looking for. The door was unremarkable, deliberately so. She checked it against the picture on her phone. This was definitely it. She glanced up. No security cameras – good. Not that she had expected them, but it was always wise to check. Her knock was answered by high-pitched barking. Tightening her grip on the strap of her rucksack, she waited.

The door was opened by a harmless-looking woman. She wore blue jeans, a non-descript sweatshirt and a smile that didn't reach her eyes. She ushered Gemma inside.

'Debbie, is it?' said the woman.

'Yes,' said Gemma.

Being careful to keep her head down, Gemma followed the woman into a back room. On the floor to the left of the door was a large, low wire enclosure. It was just high enough to keep the six French bulldog puppies contained. The barking intensified and was accompanied by squeals and snuffling as they stepped on top of each other to get a better look at Gemma. To the right of the door was a small dining table and chairs. *Perfect,* thought Gemma.

'You must be Alice,' Gemma said in a low voice.

'Yes,' said the woman. She took a breath to speak again, but Gemma had already got the answer she needed. She took Alice by the shoulders and spun her round, forcing her onto one of the dining chairs. Using a pair of zip ties, Gemma bound her arms to the chair and faced her towards the wall.

Alice was so shocked that all she could say was 'Hey!' while Gemma worked efficiently, tying Alice's feet to the legs of the chair with another pair of zip ties. Alice finally found her voice. 'What the hell are you doing?' She began to struggle, but it was too late; the ties were too tight.

'Stay quiet,' said Gemma from behind; 'someone will untie you soon.'

'Who will? What are you talking about? What's going on?' Alice began wriggling again but stopped when she realised that any more movement would topple the chair.

Gemma spotted a phone on the table. She snatched it up. 'This yours?' she said.

'Yes,' said Alice. Before she could say anything else, Gemma grabbed Alice's chin and stood close behind her to stop Alice looking around. Alice gripped the handles of the chair, her chest beginning to rise and fall rapidly. Gemma growled into her ear. 'Are you running this little operation?'

'No,' Alice replied. Gemma's close proximity had rendered her compliant – for now.

'Who then?'

'A guy called Mikey. He'll be here in an hour.'

Gemma didn't know if this was a warning or not, but it was exactly what she wanted to hear.

'I'm not going to hurt you,' said Gemma, loosening her grip and pocketing the phone. 'Just stay still. I'm going now.'

Gemma gathered up the pet carriers that lay in the adjoining kitchen and squatted by the puppies. Popping some treats from her pocket into the carriers, she lifted the pups tenderly one by one and placed them inside. When she left, one carrier in each hand, it was to the sound of Alice protesting and swearing.

She stepped into the street, biceps bulging in response to the awkward shape of the carriers. The puppies weren't heavy though. They were tiny, too small and too young to be away from their mother. She walked down a side alley and approached the car that was waiting. Placing the carriers carefully in the back seat, she buckled them in.

'Six,' she said to Carly in the driving seat. 'Three in each.'

Carly nodded, knowing they needed to keep their exchange brief.

Gemma shut the door and the car was gone, driving down one of Edinburgh's many impossibly narrow streets. Crossing the road, she became lost in the crowd again. She went a little way down the hill and waited at a bus stop. Glancing across the road at where she'd just come from, she hoped that Alice would one day get what was coming to her. She was sure this Mikey character wouldn't be too happy to find the puppies gone and no money to show for it. Those little guys would have gone for a grand a pop. As the bus arrived, she thought about what she'd done and just hoped it would serve as a warning to the puppy traders. Satisfied, Gemma jumped on the 22 and blended in with the other travellers as it trundled off down the road.

Three

The puppies made that muted squeal-whimper that puppies make while they climbed over each other with no great regard for whose foot was in whose face. They were remarkably content considering what they'd been through in their short lives, although Carly noticed that two of them were markedly quieter than the other four. Benji would be with them after work, so they'd find out the prognosis then.

Carly was seated in her wheelchair behind the computer. She was searching for known puppy farmers in the area and trying to see if there were any mentions of French bulldogs. A few months ago, there had been some evidence that French bulldogs had been coming out of a place in Fife, but there had been no whispers since. It was a possible lead, but she couldn't rule out the possibility that these puppies had come to Edinburgh from the Continent. It was rare that puppies from abroad made it as far as Scotland before being sold, but it was not unheard of. She tapped away for a few more minutes and wrinkled her brow as she did so. Every time she thought progress was being made in the area of animal welfare, they dug up something else to make her furious at humans all over again.

The government was always coming out with

piecemeal bits of legislation. They proposed reducing the hours spent in transit for live export, or they promised to reduce the number of violent abuse incidents in slaughterhouses. It simply made Carly want to shout, 'Why not just stop treating animals like they're bags of rice or cans of cola, as commodities to be bought, sold, used and abused!' She sighed and tried to focus on all the victories. But so often, abuses they thought had been eradicated became issues again, sometimes years later. Take fur, for example. In the eighties, women had paint thrown on them if they wore fur; the Animal Liberation Front blew up the fur departments of stores when they were closed at night; decent people formed a consensus that fur was A Bad Thing. Yet, here they were, the twenty-first century well established, and fashion houses were using fur again. The stars of Instagram were unashamed to be seen wearing the pelt of a fox or a coyote or a rabbit. Models paraded up and down the catwalk in London, Paris and Milan in mink, chinchilla or even dog. Real fur items had started being supplied to shops cheaply by China and nobody was objecting. Apart from a few PETA protests here and there, nobody seemed to care. *Is it time to get the paint out again?* Carly wondered.

There was a clanking at the door of their lock-up – Gemma was back.

'How are they?' was her first question. Carly was used to Gemma's abruptness.

'Fine, I think. There are two I'm a bit concerned about, but the others seem really good … considering. They barely made a peep in the car on the way down here.'

'Benji on his way?' asked Gemma.

'After work.'

Gemma turned away from Carly and bent down to inspect the puppies for herself. They were in a little play area with toys to keep them busy and shredded newspaper in case of accidents. It was thickly layered so they had no contact with the old carpet below. The first four puppies seemed perfectly normal on the surface. One circled around a few times before slouching into a heap, closing her weary eyes. Another pup stepped on her tail on his way past, but she barely stirred. Two more played by biting each other's ears and pawing gently at one another. They tumbled happily together, and Gemma allowed herself a brief smile. She could see straight away which two Carly was concerned about. They were at opposite ends of the little enclosure. Both seemed somewhat unsteady on their feet and had slightly weeping eyes. Her face darkened once again, and she stood up.

'So, what did you find out about where this little lot came from?'

'Well, it seems Fife is pretty likely. I'd say the McGregor place.' The McGregors were well known to those who fought for and supported animal rights, for all the wrong reasons. They tended to use lackeys to run their operations while they raked in the profits.

Gemma nodded. 'And homes are all sorted?'

'Yes, I think so,' said Carly, turning back to her computer. 'We've got a couple in Dumfries, one in Ayr, and the rest are in the north of England. A few weeks of love from us, and they should be strong enough to travel.'

'Good.' Gemma glanced back at the puppies.

'So ... how did it go at the house?'

'Yeah, fine,' said Gemma. 'She didn't seem too freaked out. I mean, it's not like she doesn't know she's a criminal. Got her phone.' Gemma tossed the phone onto Carly's desk. 'She said it was a bloke called Mikey that was running things.' Gemma didn't think it prudent to fill Carly in on all the details. What was the point? Carly was a full partner in their operations, but even after all this time, she still wasn't comfortable with the more physical side of things, even if it was a necessary part of dealing with scumbags.

Carly looked at the phone, checking the location was off, then at Gemma. 'There's no way you could've been seen?'

'Well, I'll have been seen but not noticed. That's the main thing. I wasn't followed. This Mikey character will be turning up any minute now, so she won't be struggling for too long.'

Carly didn't like to ask what method Gemma had used this time. She'd done everything from handcuffing people to locking them in cupboards and leaving a note. Carly trusted Gemma, but her single-minded ferocity was frightening at times. Although their methods were different, they both shared a strong moral code, and it didn't always keep them on the right side of the law.

'They hadn't even bothered with a show bitch,' said Gemma.

'Well, Frenchies are such a popular breed right now; perhaps they felt they'd be sold before anyone asked where their mum was.'

'I know what kind of hell hole they'll be keeping her in,' muttered Gemma. She had only broken into one puppy farm, but it had been an experience she'd never forget. The noise and the smell had been overwhelming. She had seen breeding bitch after breeding bitch with teats so low they scraped the filthy floor. Matted fur and sad eyes were everywhere. The cold, concrete floors were home to countless puppies, some of whom bounded around while others stared into the middle distance or shivered and shook, tiny victims of the diseases caused by lack of vaccinations and dreadful living conditions. She had wanted to scoop them all up, there and then, but had known it was impossible. So instead, she had filmed the scene with a hand that she fought to keep steady. The owners had been exposed, but one had received a measly suspended sentence, the rest had just been fined. What a joke. When she thought of the exhausted, despondent mothers in there and the poor, confused 'show bitches' who were used as display mums for the puppies in houses, she very nearly lost control. She always tried to channel that anger into action, action performed with steely determination and a drive borne out of fierce compassion and a sense of justice.

Gemma tended to the puppies, removing wet newspaper and replacing it, refilling their water and food bowls and engaging them with a bit of play. There were three boys and three girls. Two boys tugged on either end of a squeaky toy, and Gemma allowed herself to get lost in their antics.

Carly wheeled herself over and observed the scene. She hated that such innocence was exploited every day for the sake of money.

'You're an old softie at heart,' she said.

'Bugger off,' said Gemma, smiling.

***

Carly grabbed her crutches and made her way around the lock-up. Sometimes she just needed to stretch, to be in a different position. The pain hadn't been too bad today, but it was still there. It was always there. She did a circuit, feeling her joints complain then slowly ease as she walked. She was still young, but her body felt much older than her years. Dystonia was a neurological condition that plagued her with pain and uncontrollable spasms. She was lucky that her symptoms were mostly mild, but they could really spiral out of control if she was stressed or very tired. She'd worked out a system of living that minimised her symptoms, but still, she was constantly beset by pain.

Thank goodness for computers. She had been an early user of the internet and had learned to reach out to anonymous friends around the world. She'd learned hacking during the countless hours holed up in her room, too sore to play with her friends. Gemma was the one true friend who remained from those days. They'd set up all of this together, and as she wandered around the lock-up, she couldn't help feeling proud. It was a bit rough round the edges, but it worked. Her adapted car was a glorious instrument of freedom, and it had been wonderful to use it to rescue the puppies today. She smiled, perched her crutches against the wall then sat back down behind her computer. She should contact the recipients of the puppies to confirm some details.

***

Gemma needed to move. She hopped up on the treadmill they kept in the lock-up and started to pace. It was there so they could exercise dogs who came in when it wasn't safe to take them outside. Carly continued her searches on the computer, and Gemma walked to nowhere, listening to the puppies gabble. She was trim, but not thin, muscular, but not bulky. She kept fit by walking the streets of Edinburgh and occasionally running through them. Like many people, Arthur's Seat and the Crags were her favourite spots. Having that much greenery in the centre of the city was calming. On a Sunday, the road through was closed to traffic, so runners, climbers and dog walkers had the place to themselves. She enjoyed the challenge of running up the hill, taking different routes to the top and then revelling in the view of her magnificent city. Even on overcast days, the view was breathtaking. On her way down, she'd pass people with their dogs. The people would smile politely, and the dogs, off the lead, would be chasing a ball or just enjoying all the interesting smells. This gave Gemma hope. No matter how many villains she came across, she always tried to remember these people who gave their dogs names and clearly adored them, making them part of the family. These people, many of whom had probably rescued dogs from an uncertain fate, were now committed to giving them the best life they could.

The door clanked again, and in walked Benji. He carried his large vet's bag, packed with all he'd need to make a quick assessment of the puppies. Close beside him was John, a gentle mix of collie, lab and who knew what. He was three years old, the colour of sand and very much part of the team.

Benji approached Carly and gave her a kiss, while John approached the puppies in a respectful, paternal way. Gemma climbed off the treadmill as it slowed to a stop. They all joined John beside the puppies. Benji stepped into the play area and sat in a corner. He stroked one of the sick-looking puppies and picked her up. She was listless and shook a little. He murmured reassurances into her ear while he felt around her tummy and looked into her eyes and ears.

'That one's had diarrhoea,' said Gemma. Benji looked around the floor frantically. 'I cleaned it up,' she said with a wry smile.

Benji pursed his lips at Gemma and turned his attention back to the puppy.

'She's probably just dehydrated. We'll get some fluids into her and see how she gets on. There's no other sign of major illness though. Just neglect really.' He placed the pup back on the newspaper floor, and Gemma filled the water bowl nearest to her. Methodically, he picked up each pup in turn, examining them and giving advice on care. He got to the last pup whose eyes were still weeping even though Carly had cleaned them several times.

'Hmm,' said Benji, picking up the little guy. John trotted over to offer help. He sat beside them and looked concerned. They'd all heard Benji make that 'hmm' before. It was rarely a good sign.

'Well,' he said eventually, putting his stethoscope away, 'the eyes – probably just conjunctivitis like the other one. That's easily treated with ointment. It's the same stuff as humans use. However, I don't like the sound of his heart.'

They all went quiet and listened to the last pup's slightly wheezy breaths.

'He's having trouble breathing, which isn't unusual in this breed, but he seems weak too, and his heart isn't as strong as I'd expect. I think I'll have to take him in.'

John sniffed at the weak puppy and looked to Carly for guidance. She patted his head and told him he was a good boy. His tail made a single thump on the floor.

'So,' said Benji, 'where do we reckon these guys

came from?'

'It's seeming more and more likely that it's the McGregors in Fife. They've been producing lots of flat-faced breeds recently. I'll tip off the SSPCA. Gemma got a phone, but I haven't found much on it so far,' said Carly.

Flat-faced or brachycephalic breeds had broad skulls and short snouts, making both birth and breathing incredibly difficult. This recent fashion for them worried Carly immensely. Looks were lorded above all else. Many of the poor creatures were forced to endure caesareans, as there was no way for them to give birth naturally. Their lives were spent suffering from physical complications and struggling for breath.

'Yeah,' said Gemma. 'We commandeered some pugs a few months back that were from there.'

'Pugs, bulldogs, King Charles spaniels – why do people want dogs who can't breathe properly?' said Benji, exasperated.

'Cos people are dicks,' said Gemma, as though the answer was obvious.

Benji sighed, picked up the weakest of the puppies and wandered over to where the carriers had been placed. 'I think I'd better get him back to the surgery straight away.' He popped the pup into the carrier and made his way back out to his car. John remained with Carly, and she tickled him under the chin.

Gemma came over to join them. She sat on the floor in front of John and took his face in her hands. 'People are dicks, aren't they, John?' she said.

He panted happily.

Carly rolled her eyes and turned back to her computer.

Tuesday.

'Violence doesn't solve anything.' Colin McKinee gave his best, most sincere frown. The two boys sitting in front of him looked less than sincere as they nodded their heads at him. He'd given similar lectures to these two before. They were probably the most high-spirited boys in the school and were chronic in their need for sticking plasters. He hated to think what they'd be like at high school. They were worrying enough at age eight.

'Right, off you go.'

The lecture was at an end, and the boys hopped off their chairs. 'Bye Mr McKinee!' they said, swaggering out of the door. They were cheeky but mostly harmless.

Colin sighed. He shuffled some papers into a neat pile, even though everything had been dealt with for the day. His desk was incredibly tidy. It kept him calm. The bell would be sounding soon. Colin thought he might treat himself and head off a bit early today. Normally, he was the last to leave, but Miss Dalgleish was here, and she could handle things. Not that there was ever anything to handle. It was a small school, and the highest drama normally consisted of nothing more taxing than a skinned knee or a misplaced hat.

Colin waited half an hour after the bell then paid a visit to each classroom, checking to see if there was anything the staff needed before he headed off. They were all knee-deep in marking and lesson plans so most waved him away distractedly. He bade a cheery farewell to Mr Chester, the janitor, and strode out into the late afternoon sunshine.

Strolling along, his thoughts turned to his colleagues.

Had they, perhaps, been a little friendlier in days gone by? He'd only been head teacher for a year, and he'd known that there would be a social sacrifice with becoming the boss. Even before the promotion though, things hadn't been like they used to be. Over twenty years of teaching, he had seen huge changes in his profession. Idealism was reserved for the new recruits, and even then, young teachers often buckled under the pressure mere months into the job. He didn't hate his job, but it was no longer the calling it had once been. He did his best to be upbeat, but since his divorce, this had got so much tougher.

Still, he thought, *the sun is out, and I'm on my way to see Bella.* The little dog had made such a difference in his life after the divorce. He'd met her at the Edinburgh Dog and Cat Home two years ago. When he'd parked in their small car park, he hadn't been prepared for the sound of desperate barking that met his ears when he got out of his car. He'd made his way down the concrete corridor, passing jumpers, skulkers, yappers and starers. When he'd come to her run, he'd stopped. She'd been pacing around, clearly uncomfortable with her situation. The staff later told him she was a stray and very little was known about her. She was slightly smaller than a cocker spaniel with a more lightweight coat and at least three other breeds mixed in. She'd stopped pacing when she saw him. He liked to think it had been an instant connection between two lost souls. Hunkering down to her level, he had watched her wander off to find a small green ball that was lying in her run. She'd brought it to him, looking at him with utter trust, and his heart had melted. Somehow, he'd managed to get hold of the ball through the bars. He had given it a throw of sorts, and she'd caught it after one bounce. Her tail had started wagging. Mutual love was born. He'd taken her home that day.

Colin turned into his street with a feeling of relief. Bella always made life more bearable. Her relentlessly positive approach, sense of fun and unconditional love were an absolute tonic. The dog walker would have dropped her off, and she'd be at home waiting for his return, perhaps curled up on her oversized pillow bed. As he approached his house, he noticed that the side gate was open. *Odd,* he thought. He'd better close it before Bella escaped into the front garden. The house's gardens were enclosed by attractive iron fencing all round, so she couldn't get out onto the street, but he didn't want to have her barking at passers-by. She often made her way out of the doggy door at the back into the garden to sit in her favourite sunny spot beside the apple tree. Colin went in through the side gate, making sure to close it behind him, and into the back garden.

'Bella!' he called. There was no response. Her spot near the apple tree was vacant. A quick glance around told him she was not in the garden, so he fished his keys out of his pocket and unlocked the back door. He called her name again and waited to be greeted by a wagging little body desperate for pats and cuddles. The house was silent. There was no scratching on the bathroom tiles as Bella scrambled up from the cool place where she sometimes plonked herself on a warm day. There was no sound of claws against the material of her bed, or if she'd been feeling rebellious, the couch. There was no little thump when she jumped down from a chair or his bed. Colin's heart quickened. He threw his bag onto the kitchen floor and went through the whole house, stopping briefly in each room to call her name. Up the stairs, down the stairs, he looked behind every door, even under the beds. His heart was thumping hard in his chest, and he could feel his legs turning to jelly while he ran around.

'Bella!' he yelled desperately.

Colin was shaking as he punched in the dog walker's phone number. She confirmed that Bella had been dropped off as usual. He ran round to his next-door neighbour who hadn't seen Bella but had seen a suspicious van in the street half an hour earlier. This information made his stomach lurch. Other neighbours were either out or had no information. Heart still thumping, he went back to his house.

He started to sweat. He couldn't quite believe what was happening. He stumbled around once more on quaking legs checking every inch of the house. Nothing.

'BELLA!'

Silence.

With trembling fingers, Colin called the police.

Four

Carly and Gemma were having fun naming the puppies.

'This one's Muffin,' said Gemma, 'because he's shaped like a cuddly muffin.'

'You know how I feel about those kinds of names,' said Carly.

'I know, but we don't care, do we Muffin?' said Gemma, touching her nose to the little pup's.

Carly shook her head then picked up one of the girls. 'Okay, so this one's Sally, because she has the look of my cousin Sally.'

'Oops, it looks like Edina's pooped again.' Gemma rose to clean it up.

There was a ping from Carly's phone. She put Sally down with the others and looked at the screen.

'Anything interesting?' said Gemma.

'Hmm. It seems another dog's been stolen from that housing estate.' Carly brought up a map of the suburban estate on her screen. A well-to-do area, it had its fair share of thefts, but they were normally golf clubs nicked from a saloon car, not dogs from gardens. However, recently it had come up on the radar as a possible problem area when it came to missing canines.

'That's got to be the third one in as many weeks on our patch,' said Gemma, washing her hands. 'What kind was it? Smallish?'

'Yeah, cocker spaniel cross, a rescue.' Carly knew what Gemma was thinking. They'd both speculated that there was a dog-fighting ring near them somewhere after a spate of Staffie thefts had been followed by thefts of these smaller dogs.

'Perfect for a bait dog,' said Gemma, her mouth set in a grim line, all the joy of playing with the puppies gone. 'We have to look into it, Carly.'

'We don't have the resources. We're stretched as it is. It's only you, me and Benji when he's not at work.'

'And Mary,' said Gemma.

Mary was an old lady who looked as though she should work in a village post office but actually sold bongs to stoners on Cockburn Street. The range of designs for these glass smoking devices was vast, and Mary could often be seen carefully wrapping a bright green skull-shaped device or perhaps a novelty mobile phone whose antenna acted as the pipe. She also had a little drug business on the side and sometimes helped Carly and Gemma by looking after dogs at the lock-up. Mary kept quiet about their illegal activities, and they said nothing about hers.

'Okay, yes, Mary, but she's hardly much use on investigations.' Carly sighed. 'Neither am I these days.'

Gemma ignored her. 'Who's this dog's human anyway?'

'I think he's a teacher.' Carly looked at her phone. 'Colin McKinee. He seems gutted. This is definitely genuine. It says the neighbour saw a white van driving unusually fast about half an hour before the dog was discovered to be missing.'

'A white van? That's specific!'

'There's a partial plate. Very partial. Yeah, it's not much to go on. Listen, I want to help this guy as much as you do, but you can't get blood from a stone. We need more people.'

'We don't.'

'We do! You have to learn to trust people, Gemma.'

'The more people we get involved in this, the more chance we have of someone ratting us out.'

'So, we find someone who's trustworthy and who thinks that flouting the law on occasion is worth it to save animals' lives.'

'Yes,' said Gemma, scratching the head of a puppy they'd named Gerald, 'but who?'

***

Suzanne did her best to smile at the customers as they browsed around the shop. Everything glittered and shone. She'd grown used to being surrounded by jewellery, so much so that she barely saw it anymore.

'Can I help you with anything?' she said.

'No, thanks. Just looking.'

She went back behind the counter and tried not to slouch. She looked at her watch – three hours till she finished her shift. Urgh. The copious watch faces that filled the shop mocked her, even though they were all set to different times. She wasn't sure if being on her own was better or worse than having Pam, the manager, on the shop floor with her. It meant she had someone to talk to, but then celebrity gossip and the menopause were not Suzanne's favourite topics of conversation. She sighed.

Someone else entered the shop. It was a gentleman with a guide dog. Suzanne perked up. She knew she wasn't allowed to pet working dogs, but she brightened whenever she was around animals. It was only a small shop so the man found the counter before Suzanne could offer her assistance.

'Excuse me,' he said. 'I wonder if you might be able to help me?'

'Yes, of course. What can I do for you, sir?'

'Well, I'm looking for a watch for my wife. Something silver, she never wears gold.'

'Certainly. What kind of strap would suit, sir?'

He described his requirements. Suzanne got out silver watches from cabinets and guided his hands to them so he could feel the texture of each one. He had a magnifier as a feature on his phone. Suzanne was fascinated. He wanted one with a blue face, if possible. She found one in a gorgeous mid-blue that she described to him. He looked at it with the magnifier. While she was serving the man, Suzanne couldn't help glancing down towards his dog at regular intervals. The dog sat patiently for a while then decided to lie down and go to sleep. Suzanne packaged up the watch the man had decided on and asked if he'd like it gift-wrapped.

'Oh, yes, please,' he replied. 'It's for our wedding anniversary. Twenty-five years! It doesn't seem that long.' He smiled to himself, and Suzanne picked out some silver wrapping paper and silver ribbon. She was skilful at wrapping and soon had a delightful little package ready for the man. While she was helping him put it in his rucksack, his guide dog woke up.

'Is it too hot for you in here, boy?' said the man. The black lab lumbered to his feet and had a good nose to tail shake that made his harness clank.

'Your dog is gorgeous.'

'Ah, he's a good boy. He's called Chance. I can tell

you, I'm glad he took a chance on me. Just like the song!'

Suzanne couldn't help smiling. These two were adorable.

'What's your name, dear?' said the man.

'Suzanne.'

'Well, Suzanne, you've been extremely helpful.'

'Thank you, sir. You and Chance are welcome back anytime.'

'Thank you. Bye!'

She watched them leave with wistfulness. The shop was silent once again, apart from the ticking of the carriage clocks. How she longed to do work that meant something. She had had fun at university and learned a lot, but her performing arts degree seemed useless now. Work was so scarce, she supposed she should be grateful to have a job at all. She longed for the laughter and applause that she'd received performing in sketch shows and dramas. That feeling of pleasing people, cheering them up, entertaining them, was addictive, and she needed a hit. She began to put the rejected watches back in their correct places. The man with the guide dog had been lovely, but he was an exception. In this place, no matter how many times she said, 'Can I help you?' she rarely felt like she was helping anyone.

***

'What about the guy whose dog was stolen? Do you reckon he might help us get more information? Does he seem like the kind of guy who we can trust to tell us stuff but, you know, not rat us out?' Gemma raised her eyebrows at Carly.

'I don't know. I could contact him …' said Carly.

'None of the others got back to us,' said Gemma. 'I

think they thought we were dodgy.'

'We are dodgy.'

'You know what I mean. Maybe he could help us get his dog back.'

Carly turned to her computer and typed. She got alerts from all the lost dog sites and monitored all their social media that covered Scotland. 'There. I've sent him a message. I've made it sound as non-dodgy as possible while still emphasising our need for secrecy. Happy?'

'I'll be happy when we find the dogs,' said Gemma.

Carly rubbed her temples. It was all very well being the tech person, but she wished she could do more out in the field. Her dystonia presented in such a way that some days she was okay walking and some days the pain was so bad she had to resort to the wheelchair. She always kept crutches in the car though; she just didn't feel safe otherwise. Her neurological condition didn't give her any advance notice of which days she'd be well and which days she'd be in crippling agony. It was so frustrating, even after all these years, particularly as she so desperately wanted to be physically able to help Gemma catch these scumbags.

She watched Gemma play with the puppies and was reminded of how glad she was of their company when Gemma was out. The two women had been friends for years. Carly would trust Gemma with her life. They'd gone to the same primary school, and when Carly had fallen ill, it was Gemma who'd been there for her. She had visited religiously and had been a welcome distraction from the pain and discomfort. All the other kids quickly lost patience with her. Long-term illness was so isolating, and Gemma had been a light in the darkness. In later years, when Gemma experienced trauma of her own, Carly had been so glad she could be there for her, to offer the same kind of support in return.

'So, what's that one called?' asked Carly.

Gemma grinned as she stroked the little female pup whose eyes had cleared up with ointment. She seemed to be recovering well. 'I thought Squidge was a good fit.'

'Oh, for goodness sake.' Carly rolled her eyes. There was a ping, and she turned to her computer. 'That bloke's got back to us.'

'The teacher dude?' said Gemma.

'Yeah, he wants to meet up.'

There was a pause. The puppies snuffled and squeaked.

'Set it up,' said Gemma.

Carly arranged for Gemma to meet Colin the following day in a small car park off Dalry Road where they knew there was no CCTV. The reply was almost instantaneous. He'd be there.

'This guy really loves his dog. I can feel it.' Gemma touched her fist to her heart.

'He must do,' said Carly, 'to agree to meet with a dodgy bird like you.'

Five

Wednesday.

Gemma walked to the car park. She walked everywhere. She found exercise cathartic, and it was useful to keep fit. She missed having dogs to walk. The puppies were too young to go outside, unvaccinated as they were, and Benji took John to work with him. Sometimes she got to walk older dogs they'd rescued from puppy farms. That was so rewarding, because it was often the first time they'd seen grass or anything other than the inside of a barren shed. She enjoyed watching their transformation from shy and wary to outgoing and trusting. Walking and running were therapy for Gemma.

Striding along the Edinburgh streets, she grumbled internally. The pavements were uneven and shabby – totally unsuitable for a wheelchair. Gemma understood that it wasn't just her inability to run away that kept Carly from coming out into the field. Every few metres it seemed a car was parked with its tyres up on the pavement, narrowing the way through. People on crutches or with walking sticks were crowded and jostled by others. City dwellers walked fast and often bumped into less spritely pedestrians who they impatiently overtook. Not for the first time, Gemma contemplated the unfairness of life.

Aged eight, Carly had been struck down by a mystery illness. Carly, her best friend, so kind to animals and so clever, had become the victim of dystonia. They didn't even diagnose her until she was twenty. In the meantime, she'd had to put up with scans and X-rays, painful tests and broken bones due to falls. She'd sat behind a computer for most of her teenage years, learning everything there was to know about programming. She could bend the internet to her will, or so it seemed to Gemma who was mediocre at best when it came to technology. There was no justice. The number of scumbags out there, who were not only fit but thriving, made Gemma shudder with rage and loathing. She hoped she was on her way to bringing a few of those villains down.

Gemma thought about the guy she was going to meet. She knew his pain all too well. She had only been twelve when her dog, Duke, was stolen. An only child, her dog had been like a brother to her. She'd never forget the night she came home from a birthday tea out with her parents to find the back door flapping in the breeze. It had been forced open with a crowbar. The burglars had taken all of her mother's jewellery. The TV was gone. They'd even raided her piggy bank, smashing it on the floor. But all Gemma had cared about was Duke.

She'd run from room to room, shouting then screaming his name hysterically. Her parents had told the police, and they'd simply explained that the success rate in solving burglaries was very low. They advised the family to contact rescue centres and put up posters. Gemma remembered being put to bed on the night of the burglary, her parents having secured the back door with a couple of bits of wood from the garage. She'd lain in her bed, too frightened to go to sleep, getting up at every creak or unexplained noise, hoping it was Duke scratching at the door, but it never was. Each time, she would pad back to her bedroom and stare out of the window onto the street, hoping to see him appear from behind a hedge. Nobody got much sleep that night. The insurance covered all the missing things, but Duke wasn't a thing. He wasn't an item to be replaced.

They'd searched desperately for a year. Gemma had put up posters on lamp posts, as many as she could. When they got ragged from the weather or torn down, she'd replace them with new ones. They'd even offered a substantial reward. After the search was abandoned, Gemma's parents tentatively suggested that they get another dog, but she couldn't even contemplate it. She still dreamed that, one day, he'd come back. Her constant hope was that he'd run away from the frightening men who'd broken into his house and got lost. Perhaps some lovely family had found him and given him a home. He didn't have a microchip, so maybe he had ended up somewhere too far away for his new family to have seen the posters.

As she'd got older, she began to learn about men who stole dogs for money, to use in dog fights. Nightmares about Duke in such a scenario had followed, crowding her sleep, no matter how hard she tried to block the images from her mind. She had never learned Duke's fate, and the uncertainty still haunted her. When her parents had died four years later, struck by a white BMW doing eighty miles per hour down the wrong side of a country road, she'd fallen apart. A year went by where nobody had been able to get through to her, not Carly and not even her doting grandparents, who were grief-stricken themselves. It was after that she'd got in with the wrong crowd. Even though she'd eventually let Carly back into her life, she'd made countless mistakes during that time. But she'd toughened up and, finally, around seven years later, pulled herself together. Her parents weren't coming back, so she forced herself to get on with her life. From then on, she swore she'd use her considerable inheritance to get justice for dogs like Duke who had had their lives turned upside down by criminals. Everything she did was for him and for her parents. She hoped that, wherever they were, they understood the risks she had to take, the rules she had to bend and that they were proud.

Gemma's determined strides eventually took her to the car park. She spotted him straight away. Although very ordinary-looking, this was not a man used to trying to blend in. The nervous look on his face gave him away instantly. His eyes darted around, taking in every shopper coming or going, looking for her. She approached him casually.

'Hi Colin.'

'Are you …?'

'Yes. My associate contacted you through the lost dog appeal you posted. We're very keen to help you find Bella, along with some other dogs who've been stolen from the area.'

'Others?'

'Yes, but before I go into too much detail, I must stress again that we're not an official organisation.'

Colin nodded, saying nothing.

Gemma continued. 'We operate … independently of the authorities. Going through official channels can be slow, and we believe that Bella may have been stolen by some fairly hardened criminals.'

Colin whimpered. 'I told the police, but they just said—'

Gemma could see the emotion in his eyes, and her determination grew stronger. 'To call local rescue centres and put up posters, I know. We believe Bella was taken by a gang who may be involved in dog fighting, but I can't say anything for sure just yet. I can assure you that you won't be implicated in any illegal activity; we just want to find your dog. Is there any information you can give me that wasn't in your original post?'

Colin had gone pale. 'She's only a small dog. What use would she be to'—he swallowed hard—'dog fighters? They must use Staffies or pit bulls, breeds like that, surely?'

'I'm sorry to say that bait dogs are used to train the traditional fighting breeds.' She clocked the horrified look on his face. 'Let's not get into that though, Colin. We're determined to find her. Please tell me anything else you can think of that might be of help.'

'My neighbour saw a white van outside my house when she was walking her own dog, about half an hour before I got home from work. She knew it wasn't the dog walker's van as that's blue and has paw prints painted on the side.'

'Was there anything distinctive about it? Anything at all.'

'Well, I put the partial number plate she'd remembered in the post online.' Colin seemed to be searching his brain. 'Oh, there was one thing she said. She said it had a sticker in the side window, a sticker with hedgehogs on.'

'Hedgehogs?' said Gemma urgently.

'Yes, one of those horrible ones that have lots of hedgehogs, some crossed out like they're keeping score of how many they've run over.'

Gemma snatched her phone from her pocket. Clamping it to her ear, she instinctively laid a hand on Colin's shoulder. 'We'll be in touch,' she said, looking him straight in the eyes and giving him what she hoped was a reassuring nod. She strode away, and he stayed where he was, watching her go.

Carly picked up. 'Carly,' she barked, 'I think it's the McGregors.'

'The puppies?' said Carly.

'No, not the puppies.' Gemma began to jog. 'Well, maybe the puppies, but I think they've been stealing the dogs. Seems like they're not just puppy farmers. Yeah, see what you can find online. I'll be back soon to pick you up. We're going to Fife.'

***

Gemma entered the lock-up at a run. She stopped short when she saw a stranger there.

'Who's this?' she said to Carly, panting slightly.

'This is Suzanne; she's Benji's cousin.'

'And where is he? And what about Mary?'

'You'll have to forgive Gemma's bluntness,' said Carly to Suzanne, who stood there looking a bit awkward.

'It's fine,' said Suzanne. 'I'm here to look after the puppies. I just love dogs.' She smiled at Gemma, who gave a grim nod in return.

'Benji's at work, Mary's … erm … indisposed and Suzanne has kindly stepped in on her day off.'

'Oh right,' said Gemma. Then as an afterthought,

'Thanks.'

'Right,' said Carly, 'I'm feeling okay today, so I might just take my stick with me.' She was patting pockets to search for keys and checking her rucksack for all the essentials. 'So, I've got your number, you've got mine, and don't worry, they're absolute darlings.'

'No problem.'

'Don't phone unless it's an emergency,' said Gemma.

Carly gave her a stern look, and Gemma gave a shrug of her shoulders that said, *What?*

'Right, that's us away. We should be back by teatime, but there are sandwiches and juice in the fridge. Help yourself.'

'Thanks very much. The puppies will be fine.' She directed this last remark at Gemma who was still looking a bit scary.

With that they went outside, bundled themselves into the car and were off.

***

'What does she know?' said Gemma while they worked their way towards the A90.

'Not much,' said Carly, keeping her eyes on the road. 'You could've been a bit nicer in there.'

'I was taken by surprise!'

They drove in silence for a while, but as the Forth bridges rose before them, Carly started talking.

'I can't believe they could be into dog fighting too.'

'I know,' said Gemma.

She knew that Bella, being a cross-breed, was totally useless in the puppy farming industry. People wanted designer dogs. At the moment, that meant handbag-sized, with flat faces. Pugs and French bulldogs were currently the most popular. The whole dog-breeding scene disgusted Gemma. Forcibly breeding dogs then selling them for money was just commercialised canine eugenics. Over centuries, people had bred the domestic dog to suit their own needs. There were those bred as companions or lap dogs, like chihuahuas and King Charles spaniels, or for attacking other animals, like bulldogs and boxers. Of course, there were many, many other functions dogs had been bred for over the years such as hunting assistants or sheep herders, but it was the first two motivations that seemed to be alive and well and being facilitated in Fife.

The McGregors were notorious. A husband-and-wife team, they'd been laughing at the law for years. Well known in animal rights circles, they commercialised animal abuse in the form of puppy farming but always managed to get away with it. The law was lax in the field of dog breeding. The McGregors made their bitches have litter after litter, even though it was illegal to allow a bitch to have more than five litters a year without a special licence. Premises were rarely checked. Gemma and Carly both knew that, even if puppy farmers did get caught breaking the law, they'd get a suspended sentence and an insignificant fine. The best result they could get would be a ban for life from keeping animals, but as the McGregors often had other people front their operations, this was unlikely. Even if, by some miracle, the police did catch them, the law was known to be poorly enforced and neglect or abuse would have to be proven to make a case stick. *Well,* thought Gemma, *when it comes to bending the law, two can play at that game.*

'I mean it has to be that, or else what's the point of

stealing a full-grown dog. It's not like they're going to sell her to anyone,' said Carly, almost afraid to contemplate the awfulness of it all.

'Of course. People might sell a puppy, but a four-year-old cross-bred bitch? No way. She's being used as a bait dog, no question in my mind.'

'Well, hopefully not yet, if we get to her in time.' Carly sped up slightly. 'Did you explain to the guy what a bait dog was?'

'To Colin? No, not really. He was pretty traumatised as it was, so I thought I'd leave it till we knew for sure.'

Carly had found footage of bait dogs in action on the Dark Web. It had been a truly disturbing sight. They were used as sparring partners for the more powerful pit bulls and were subject to terrible abuse, often having teeth removed to make them even more powerless, so the fighting dogs could gain confidence and get more aggressive. Bait dogs ended up with horrific injuries, and those who'd been rescued, often showed signs of lasting psychological damage. The others ended up dead. Carly and Gemma had watched terrified, vulnerable dogs being literally thrown at bigger, stronger dogs who were teased and trained to kill them. The fighting dogs were also abused horribly, not acting according to their will. They were forced to attack or face death themselves. All this so that men, sadly it was almost always men, could bet money on which dog would kill and which would die. Although dog fighting had been banned in the UK for over two hundred years, it still went on, lurking in the shadows, a threatening figure from the past.

They were on the country roads now, having left the motorway behind. Gemma had only been to the McGregors' once, but she could remember the way perfectly. She directed Carly, and when they saw the massive shed at the end of a dirt track, they stopped. There didn't appear to be anyone around, but appearances could be deceiving.

'There's a clearing about a quarter of a mile up the road where we can hide the car. You up for walking?'

Carly nodded. She was feeling strong today, and the thought of finding out what had happened to Bella and the other missing dogs was driving her on. They dumped the car and made their way towards the shed through some long grass to the side of it. The grass was so long that it almost reached Carly's shoulders. Under their feet, the ground was uneven, in the way that lumpy mud goes when it dries in the heat. Carly was doing her best, but she began to wish she'd brought her stick with her instead of leaving it in the car. As they got closer, they could hear the barking that couldn't be heard from the road.

'That sounds like a lot of dogs,' said Carly, grimacing from both dread and effort.

'It does.'

They continued towards the shed, crouching slightly as they got nearer. There was a small side building that they'd have to pass to reach the dogs. Gemma motioned for Carly to stay in cover while she crept over to it. She ducked under the window and got her phone out. Putting it in camera mode, she slid it up so the lens poked up just over the window sill. Tilting the phone slightly, she checked out the image of the little office from her place of safety and saw that the room was empty but the door was open. There was paperwork that looked tantalisingly like it could contain evidence on the desk beside the window.

Gemma motioned to Carly that it was safe to move.

She crept over to join Gemma.

'There's a bunch of papers on that desk that could give us some information.'

'You go in; I'll be a lookout?' Carly looked slightly pained. The crouching was becoming an effort.

'Yup,' said Gemma.

She went the long way round the back of the shed to the door, so as not to be seen from the front. Carly followed her. Gemma entered the office and went straight to the desk, while Carly stood just inside the door, peeking round it so she could see if anyone was coming. It was an outhouse of an office, its stone walls giving it a cold atmosphere, even on such a warm day. Gemma took out her phone and started taking pictures. There were various notes and receipt books which she photographed, all designed to make the business look legitimate. The desk was messy though, and she moved a few things to get a proper look at everything. There was disappointingly little detail about the dogs themselves. The receipts listed either 'pup' or 'dog' or 'bitch' and an amount of money beside each one. Once again, animals treated as commodities. The numbers she saw were within the legal limits, but she guessed they were hiding a lot more breeding bitches and puppies behind the cosy facade. Nothing she saw gave her any indication that dog fighting was on the agenda. Once she'd finished with the desk, she looked around the walls. They were mostly bare. There was just a staff schedule and a picture of the McGregors with a local businessman. They had their fingers in many pies. Animal abuse was their speciality though, and she dreamed of bringing them down one day. While she was photographing the items on the walls, Carly dashed into the office.

'He's coming!'

Gemma made for the door but was blocked by Carly who simply said, 'Too fast, too fast!' and hid behind the open door.

Gemma had known her friend long enough not to argue. She looked around desperately. There wasn't room for them both behind the door. Her eyes fell on the desk, which was large and very deep. She scrambled under it just as she heard someone enter the office. All she could see was a pair of large work boots that stomped towards the desk, filling her with dread. She heard a shuffle of papers. He was searching around on the desk for something. Had she put everything back where it had been? She didn't know. After what seemed like an age, he walked away from the desk, and Gemma saw the bottom of overalls. Probably the person employed to feed the puppies. Just when she thought he was about to leave, the boots came back towards her. Only this time, an uncomfortable-looking desk chair was being dragged towards the desk. Her heart quickened. *If he sits down,* thought Gemma, *we're done for. There's no room for his legs plus me under here.* The chair was plonked in front of the desk. Gemma tensed for action.

Six

The sound of tyres on gravel made the boots stop still. Gemma held her breath. Suddenly, the boots walked briskly out of the door. Gemma exhaled and scrambled out from under the desk. She hurried over to Carly by the door and found that her friend was shaking. Gemma laid a hand on her arm.

'That was too close,' said Carly. Gemma made her way over to the tiny front-facing window and looked out. She could see two men getting out of a silver Audi, being greeted by overalls man, who she could now see was very large indeed. Even with Gemma's level of fighting skill, she was glad she hadn't had to confront him.

She ran a commentary for Carly. 'There are a couple of blokes getting out of a flash car, and they're handing one of those big trug things to the guy who was just in here. He's dumping it round the corner on our side of the big shed. Okay, one of them's going in the shed at the front with our man, and the other one's just sparked up a fag and is waiting by the car.'

'Can we just head out the way we came in?'

'Nah. Cigarette man would see us. He's got a good view of the fields. Let's sneak over and see what's in that trug.'

'Gemma—' But before Carly could finish, Gemma

was tiptoeing over to the bucket, which was out of sight of cigarette man. Carly reluctantly followed. The large plastic bucket was black and scuffed – the kind one might use for gardening. Gemma's face was set in a scowl. Carly caught up to her. They could both see what was in the bucket now, and it was not a pretty sight. Lying in the bottom, tossed in like so much rubbish, were seven dead puppies, no more than a couple of weeks old. Their little bodies lay motionless in different positions. You could almost believe they were just asleep – if it was not for their still little bellies and their morbidly pale skin. They were too young to discern what breed they were. Sadness that they'd never grow up hit both women. Gemma felt the bile rise up in her stomach, her anger along with it. Carly noticed.

'We can't let them spot us,' she whispered, laying a hand on Gemma, steadying her.

'I know,' said Gemma. She knew she was quick to anger, but quite honestly, she'd challenge anyone not to feel rage at a sight like this. Taking out her phone, she photographed the little bodies. Suddenly, they heard voices.

'Any problems?' said a voice.

'Nah,' said a deeper voice, possibly overalls man. 'I've got a bird coming to see the Westies at four o'clock. They've been selling like hotcakes.'

'Good,' said a third voice. 'We'll have some cockapoos coming over from Ireland in the next few days. They should go quickly too. Plus, you can charge more for them. The Westies are six hundred, but the cockapoos will go for at least eight.'

'No bother,' said overalls.

'Now, about that other matter. Do you have the site

all set up for Saturday?'

'Yup, the container at the docks. Nobody goes round there at any time, least of all the cops. It's just waste ground.'

'We'll have a code question to get in.'

'What is it?'

'You'll like this Mikey. It's: Did you see the match last night? And the answer is: Partick Thistle won.'

There was laughter. Gemma and Carly heard the crunching of gravel as the two men made their way to the car.

'I'm bringing the dogs from Livingston, and Stan's got two new ones he's trying out. I'll bring along some of the baits to get them psyched up.'

'Okay. See you around seven.'

'See you then, Greg.'

With that they heard the men getting into the Audi and the car's engine start up. Worryingly, they also heard the crunch of big boots on gravel coming towards them. Gemma and Carly knew they had to move quickly or he would see them for sure. They dashed round the back of the big shed and miraculously found a door open. Ducking inside, they observed overalls man walk away from them. He made his way back into the office, and they dared to breathe again.

Looking around, they found that they were standing on a cold, concrete floor, a small fence dividing them from what must have been a hundred puppies and their mothers. There was no bedding, no straw, just bare floor covered in urine. They could see that some of the dogs' paws had become red and inflamed through contact with the ammonia. The stench of waste and neglect stung as they breathed it in. Most of the mothers lay in corners or near the wall, seemingly seeking some sort of refuge from this living hell. Their teats hung low, and some were so dirty that it was obvious they'd been here for a while and had birthed many litters. Gemma was transported back to the last time she'd investigated this place. She had been able to do nothing then except film the horror and hope for justice. Feeling equally helpless now, she still took out her phone to film the conditions. Would anyone care about this even if it was exposed? They hadn't before.

'We have to get them out,' said Carly. 'We have to shut this place down.' She was taking pictures with her phone. She couldn't resist gently stroking some of the mothers, even though most cowered away from her touch.

'You know what the law's like,' said Gemma, more harshly than she'd intended.

Carly let it wash over her. 'Surely people can't come here thinking this is a great place to buy a puppy?'

Gemma didn't reply. Instead, she stepped over the fence, still filming, being careful to avoid the dogs and the poop in the dark. She walked towards the front of the shed and slowly opened a door to see where it led. Despite the rage that fuelled her desire to fight with relish if caught, she still peered through with caution before walking through. After all, Mikey, the overalls man, would present quite the David and Goliath match. The horrific smell dissipated. On the other side of the door was a much smaller dog enclosure with far fewer dogs. Natural light streamed in from the front, and Gemma had to blink her eyes as they adjusted. There was a litter of West Highland terrier puppies but no mother that Gemma could see. Carly caught up to her.

'I wish you'd stop wandering off like that,' she said. She looked around her at the glass panelling and the shredded newspaper. 'So, this is the shop front, I suppose.' She shut the door they'd just come through. 'Goodness, it's amazing how much that muffles the sound from back there, isn't it?'

Gemma nodded. They observed the puppies. There were nine of them.

'Westies normally have between three and five puppies,' said Carly. 'These must be from different litters.'

'Yeah,' said Gemma.

An untrained eye would see nothing wrong with the puppies, but she observed that they weren't nearly as playful as puppies normally were at that age. She also knew they were too young to be away from their mother.

'Scum,' she said, under her breath.

She took some pictures with her phone. As she did so, the sound of heavy boots on gravel came through the open front door. Quickly, they retraced their steps, careful to shut the door quietly behind them. They made their way, weaving through the puppies, to where they'd first entered the shed. They were about to leave by that door, when they saw Mikey's shadow moving towards them. Pressing themselves to the wall near the door, they prayed he wouldn't see them. He walked past the open door, carrying the trug the other men had left for him. He headed away towards the back of the property, probably towards some dumping site.

'Let's go,' said Gemma, but Carly was slumped against the wall, face contorted in pain.

'I can't run. I'm having a massive spasm,' she said. 'You go.'

'No way,' said Gemma. At the end of the little walkway they were on, she spotted a storeroom. Pointing at it, she said, 'We'll hide in there till you recover.' Not waiting on an answer, she hoisted Carly up and half carried her to the storeroom. It was fairly roomy, and Carly sunk down on a large bag of dog food. They were positioned to the left of the door so nobody could see them from the outside. Gemma got down beside Carly.

'Is there anything I can do? Muscle massage?'

'No,' said Carly, her leg twitching and kicking out. 'Just have to wait for it to pass.'

Gemma felt powerless. They both just sat there for a moment, Carly's body still twisting and spasming, making the dry dog food rustle and crunch beneath her. Gemma so wanted to help her friend. She always had, ever since they were kids. It suddenly occurred to Gemma that she should perhaps shut the storeroom door, but then she thought better of it, as Mikey might notice something was different. They sat in relative silence, even though any sound they made would be drowned out by the barking. Then it happened. The boots, this time stomping on cold concrete, coming right towards them. Carly jumped violently when Mikey bellowed at the dogs to shut up. Gemma leapt up. He'd be coming in here for dog food. She had to try to defend them, even though she knew she stood little chance against the giant of a man, especially with her friend in spasm and their car so far away. They were out of sight, but they soon wouldn't be.

***

There was no warning as the trug, now empty, flew into the storeroom. No giant appeared, but as soon as the bucket landed on the floor, the door slammed shut, and they heard a key work in the lock. The boots tramped away, and Carly looked at Gemma who was still standing, positioned like some sort of ninja.

'We're screwed, aren't we?' she said. Instead of replying, Gemma simply slumped down beside her friend and put her head in her hands.

There was a little window, with an old-fashioned net curtain over it, so at least they had some light. Carly found herself wondering why a storeroom would have a net curtain.

They were surrounded by everything you'd expect to find in a facility that kept dogs – bags of food, leashes, food and drink bowls, towels, a big box of shredded newspaper, a shit shovel. There were also a few things you really wouldn't expect to be there. Hanging from the back of the door were three thick, wooden sticks, tapered at one end. Two of them had blood spatters on them. Carly now knew why this storeroom's contents were being hidden behind net curtains and a locked door.

'Prying sticks,' she said.

'What?' said Gemma, lifting her head up.

Carly pointed. 'There are prying sticks on the back of this door. You know, for separating dogs at dog fights.'

While Gemma took pictures, Carly thought about the footage she'd watched of dogs' jaws being prised apart with these crude implements. Sometimes the dogs became so frenzied that they simply wouldn't let go of their opponent, so these sticks were forced into their mouths like a crowbar.

'And,' Carly continued, 'I can see some pretty heavy-looking chains.' The chains were coiled up under a low shelf. They'd been invisible from standing height but were perfectly visible when you were sitting on a bag of dog food on the ground. Carly got up from her seated position while Gemma photographed the chains. She stretched and felt the flow of adrenaline slow a little. The spasm was over for now, so she was left with pain, discomfort and a desperate desire to find a way out.

'No wonder he's locked the door,' said Carly. 'If he's got someone coming round to look at those Westies, he can't risk them stumbling across this little lot.' She pointed at the prying sticks again. 'He's probably locked the door to this back area too, so they don't see where they breed them.' Carly bit her lip as she thought of the possibility there might be more than one locked door lying between them and freedom.

'What are these?' said Gemma. She was holding up medicine bottles that she'd found while rummaging around behind some collars.

Carly took a good look at the label. 'Steroids. They'd never be needed in a place that was just focused on dog breeding, and anyway, you wouldn't have them just lying around if you had a legitimate use for them. A vet would prescribe them.'

'You only have to look around to see they don't give a shit about their dogs' health here,' said Gemma, getting a photo of the bottle.

'Yeah, those steroids can be injected into the fighting dogs' muscles to enhance their performance. This is all the evidence we need to spark an investigation, more than enough.'

'If we can get them on the illegal conditions in this place and on dog-fighting charges, they might even do some time,' said Gemma with a hopeful look on her face.

'Yes,' said Carly, 'but there's just one snag.'

'What's that?'

'We need to break out of this place first.'

Gemma's face fell. 'Oh yeah.' She was quiet for a second. 'Do you know what though? I reckon I recognised those guys from the Audi just now. I'm sure I've seen them at one of the McGregor trials. They're lackeys of theirs.'

'Yeah, their names seemed familiar.' Carly took out her phone. No signal. She waved it around a bit and found that she got a very weak signal near the net-curtained window. She brought up a photograph from a newspaper report from the previous year. The McGregors were pictured marching out of court, triumphant after receiving a modest fine for animal abuse. In the background, the men who had called each other Stan and Greg were plain to see.

Gemma looked at the picture and nodded. 'The McGregors run multiple puppy farms, so those guys must have brought the dead puppies from one of their other places.'

'One that doesn't have such a convenient dumping site,' said Carly. Grimacing at the memory, she started tapping at her phone again. She called Benji, thinking that perhaps he could come to the property and pretend to be on a routine inspection or something. The phone rang and rang and finally went to voicemail. Next, she tried his vet practice. Rose, the receptionist answered and said that Benji had just gone into surgery and wouldn't be out for another hour or so. Nobody else at the practice knew what Benji did on the side. It was his surgery, so there was nobody superior to him to question his motives. It meant, though, that asking anyone else there for help was out of the question.

'We could call Mary,' suggested Gemma.

'Mary? She'd be of no help. Although …' Carly rang Mary. She was finished with whatever shady business she was up to in Edinburgh and was on her way home. Carly asked her to go to the lock-up and look after the puppies. She readily agreed.

'Why did you ask her to look after the puppies?' said Gemma. 'Isn't the new girl doing that?'

'Yes,' said Carly and dialled Suzanne's number.

***

Suzanne was in her element. She'd had babysitting jobs before, but this was much more fun than reading a bedtime story and then sitting watching telly all evening. She had played gentle tug-of-war games with the puppies using empty toilet rolls. When they had tired of tug of war, they sat down and shredded the cardboard with their needle-like teeth. Suzanne then threw little balls for them, which they chased, pushing their wee legs to the limit. Their little bodies had eventually grown tired, and she had sat on the floor watching them fall asleep one by one.

She was just taking out her phone to take pictures of their angelic little faces when it rang. It was Carly. She answered it and listened intently.

Carly and Gemma were in a spot of bother. *Uh-huh.* They were trapped in a storeroom on a puppy farm. *Um, a what?* It didn't matter, but they needed her to create a distraction so they could break out. *But I'm looking after the puppies!* Mary would be along in a minute to take over. She was given the directions to the farm and was told to pretend to be looking to buy Westie puppies. BUT whatever she did, she was not to buy one. Stall, stall, stall. Carly and Gemma were locked in a storeroom at the back of the building, with no keys to get out. If there were keys, maybe Suzanne could steal them? *What? Why were they there in the first place?*

'No time to explain, just get here. We can't risk the big guy who runs the place seeing us escape.' *But why ...?* 'Please,' Carly pleaded, 'just come and help us, and we'll pay you five times what we paid you to look after the puppies. It's got to be before four o'clock, because that's when the real person who's coming to buy a puppy is coming.' *The real person?* 'Please, just come. If he's inside the front of the building with you, he won't notice us, but if he's in the office, where he probably is at the moment, he will!'

Carly hung up. Suzanne sat staring at the innocent puppies, marvelling at the criminality that had brought them into this world.

Suzanne had got a good idea of the layout of the place from Carly's description. Her heart pounded while she digested this news. She went over to the desk and found some spare paper and a pen. With a slightly shaky hand, she wrote down the directions to the farm while they were fresh in her mind. She also wrote down *Westie puppies – Don't buy* and *Storeroom at the back*. She looked at her watch. If she left very soon, she should get there on time. Her mind was racing. Moments later, an old woman in a tweed skirt, a sensible blouse and pale blue cardigan entered the lock-up. Her hair looked to be made of cotton wool, and she wore the most comfortable-looking shoes Suzanne had ever seen. She looked like a total blast from the past. The old woman introduced herself as Mary.

'Lovely to meet you, Mary,' said Suzanne, extending a hand.

Mary shook it. 'Oh, look at the little dears; they look

absolutely puggled.'

It was a word, meaning tired out, that Suzanne's grandmother often used, and it immediately warmed her to Mary.

'Yes, we've been playing,' said Suzanne, smiling.

'Good, good,' said Mary and settled down on a chair overlooking the sleeping pups. 'Well, you'd better be off. I hear the girls have got themselves into a bit of trouble.'

Suzanne was unsure of how much she should discuss what she'd been asked to do, so she merely nodded and smiled as Mary got her knitting out of her bag. Fetching her own bag, Suzanne shoved her notes in it and headed for the door. She said goodbye, and Mary waved her knitting. Heading to her little car, Suzanne couldn't help thinking, *What weirdness have I got myself into?*

Seven

'What time is it now?' said Gemma, pacing about.

Carly looked at her watch. 'Just after three.' She had been searching for information on her phone, figuring she may as well use their time for something useful. Her phone could be used to access her computer back at the lock-up. She beckoned Gemma over to look at the screen.

Gemma's mouth fell open. 'Mikey is their son?' she said.

'Yup,' said Carly, triumphant. 'It seems we're currently accidentally imprisoned by none other than Mikey McGregor.'

'I don't remember him for any of their trials,' said Gemma.

'No,' said Carly, 'it seems he's been keeping a low profile. Though, from what we've heard today, it appears he knows about everything that's going on. He's sure to have access to all their dealings. There's no way that he's just a lowly dog feeder. I can't believe I didn't put this together before. The name Mikey meant nothing to me in connection to that woman, Alice, and her phone. I'm even more glad you picked it up when rescuing the wee Frenchies now. More evidence.' Carly looked towards the window. 'If only we could get access to a computer here ... or his phone.'

'I didn't see a computer on the desk when we were in the office,' said Gemma. 'And I can't exactly rummage in his pockets from here—'

'It also seems that the guys called Greg and Stan may be involved in gangster activity in Edinburgh – if it's the same Greg and Stan.' Carly stretched her back, stiff and tired from craning towards the little window for signal.

They had discussed how they could break out. Among some old tools in a corner, they'd found a crowbar, but if they broke the door, Mikey would be alerted that someone had been there.

'We can't have them know we were here,' said Gemma, biting her nails. 'We've got to keep it covert.'

'Well, we don't have much choice,' said Carly. 'He locked us in. And chances are, the next time that door opens, he'll come in looking for something and may just notice two strange women in his storeroom.'

'I know, but if they know we've been here, they'll know someone's been digging about, and they'll hide the evidence that links them to the dog fighting ring. Let's face it, it's a far more serious offence and harder to explain away than the poor pups through there.' Gemma jerked her thumb in the direction of the dogs. Her mind flickered onto thoughts of Duke, her childhood friend, but she pushed the thoughts away. 'How do we know we can trust this girl?'

'Suzanne is Benji's cousin. She's a lovely girl who adores animals and is at a bit of a loose end in life. She works in a jewellery shop.'

'Yes, but how do we know we can trust her?' Gemma said again.

Carly folded her arms and sighed.

Gemma went back to pacing. It had always been her

and Carly, just doing the best they could to save puppies from a cruel trade. The two of them worked well together; they knew each other's foibles and could anticipate each other. When Carly had met and married Benji, before they'd got the lock-up and started saving puppies, Gemma had felt frozen out. The feeling had only been temporary though. And when they'd decided to use Gemma's inheritance to buy the lock-up and fund their little schemes, it had made Carly feel useful and Gemma feel whole again.

Carly's disability meant she didn't have the consistency of health needed for a permanent job, so she had been delighted to use her skills to research everything for the two of them. She had found ways of getting in touch with other individuals who supported animal rights, who understood their need to bend the rules in order to get justice. She also investigated cases of abuse or neglect, but they mainly rehabilitated puppies and breeding bitches rescued from horrific operations like the one they were currently trapped in. Loving homes were found for poorly puppies and tired-out mothers alike.

For the past five years, both Gemma and Carly had gained a real sense of self-worth from making a difference in the world. But now, Gemma wanted to expand operations and Carly had made it clear that they couldn't do that, not without more people. Gemma felt they could. She was wary of Suzanne, as she was of anyone outside their tight little circle. She'd learned to accept Benji, and Mary never asked questions, but it had always been just her and Carly, and that's how she wanted things to stay. Experience had told her that, in general, you could trust animals instantly, but humans had to really earn it.

'She's going to screw up, then we'll all be in the shit,' said Gemma.

'What makes you think that?'

'She's so young and … and naive.'

'You weren't naive at that age. Neither was I. I was only a year older than her when Benji and I got married.'

'That's different. We'd been through stuff.' Gemma was still pacing around. 'We knew what to expect from other people. She works in a shop for God's sake.'

'You worked in a shop,' said Carly mildly.

Gemma opened her mouth to say something but knew that her voice would rise to a shout, and they couldn't afford to be discovered because of her temper.

Carly looked amused. 'Look, she's Benji's cousin. She has no reason to betray us—'

'That you know of,' interjected Gemma.

Carly ignored her. 'She loves animals. She knows what they're doing here is wrong, and she wants to help us. She's a steady girl. I'm sure she won't mess up.' Carly put her hand on Gemma's leg as her friend passed to stop her pacing. 'She's on our side.'

'Well, she'd better hurry up,' said Gemma, grabbing the crowbar off its hook on the wall.

***

Suzanne pulled up in front of the large shed and sat in the car. She had intended taking a moment to gather her thoughts and text Carly to let her know she'd arrived, but straight away, a very large man wearing overalls and hulking boots appeared, striding towards her. Her heart began to quicken, but she took a deep, calming breath, just as she used to do before a big drama performance. She wound down the window.

'Here to get a puppy?' he said, with what he obviously thought was a smile.

'Yes,' said Suzanne brightly. She then remembered her instructions. 'Well, I'm here to have a look, at least.'

She got out of the car and followed the man through the front door of the shed. She looked around the space. It had a concrete floor then, behind a Perspex partition in an area covered in shredded newspaper, were some adorable West Highland terrier puppies. The man slung one leg then the other over the low partition to join the puppies. He gave her an eager look. 'So, which one do you want then?'

It was at this point that it struck Suzanne as odd that he hadn't introduced himself. He hadn't asked her for her name either. Anonymous transactions were obviously de rigueur in this place. She blinked and looked at the puppies. They looked so vulnerable, especially with this big dolt standing among them. She had to find a way to contact Carly.

'Do you mind if I take photos of them?' She got out her phone.

'I'd rather you didn't,' said the man.

'Oh, it's just that I promised my husband that I would … to let him see the new family pet, you know.'

'You can take it home today,' said the man.

'Well, it's just he is paying—'

'They're all pretty much the same,' said the man, gesturing around.

Suzanne pretended to appraise the puppies while she desperately tried to think of a stalling tactic. The huge man's indignant look was putting her off. 'Um, could I use your toilet?' she said eventually. 'It was a bit of a drive here.'

'Fine,' said the man and made to get out of the pen to show her where it was.

'Oh no,' said Suzanne quickly, 'don't put yourself out. Just tell me where it is, and I'll find it. I won't be long.'

'It's next to the office building.' He pointed in the direction he'd come from.

'Thank you,' said Suzanne, giving a little smile. 'I won't be long,' she said again.

Making her way out of the big shed, she strode towards the little office. With a quick glance behind her, she ducked into the office and looked for keys. She hurried over to the desk and opened drawer after drawer. Nothing. She looked on the desk itself and around the walls. He must have them on him. *Damn!* She should text Carly. She'd do it from the toilet, so she didn't get caught in here. As she was exiting, she had a quick glance behind the door, and there, on a hook on the wall, was a small bunch of keys. *Bingo!*

Grabbing them, she ran to where Carly had described, glancing again in the direction of the front door. The door to the back of the shed had been closed and locked, but she opened it with one of the keys. On entering, she could immediately see why the man was so keen to hide what was inside. Suzanne gasped at the pitiful sight that greeted her. The barking and the smell and the depressing vision of countless dogs in a disgusting state almost floored her, but she knew she had to remain focused. There was no time to process it all. She tore herself away from the horror and located the storeroom door. There were two big keys that looked like they'd fit. She tried the first – no good. She tried the second, praying this was the one. It was a bit clunky in the lock but turned with some persuasion. The door creaked open, drowned out by the din of barking, and there, with a crowbar in her hand, was a very aggressive-looking Gemma.

'Where is he?'

'At the front with the Westies, but I'd better get back.'

Carly appeared. 'Thanks so much! When we didn't get a text, we thought—'

'I went for the keys. That way he won't know you've been here.' Carly raised her eyebrows and cocked her head at Gemma. 'Speaking of which,' said Suzanne, 'I'd better lock this behind you and return the keys.'

Carly and Gemma exited the cupboard while Suzanne locked up.

'What will I say when I go back there. I can't just drive away, or he'll know something's up,' said Suzanne.

'Just say you don't have the money on you,' said Carly; 'that's all they're interested in.'

'Okay.'

They made their way to the other door quickly and quietly. As Suzanne locked it behind them, she looked at Gemma's worried face and said, 'Don't worry, I've got this.'

Gemma nodded. She motioned that it was clear, and she and Carly ran towards the fields. Carly looked over her shoulder at Suzanne and made praying hands, mouthing, 'Thank you.'

Suzanne returned the keys to the office and crept out. She saw cigarette smoke wafting from the direction of the front door. She stood there, watching it curl and disappear on the breeze. She'd been so focused on getting Carly and Gemma out that she hadn't had time to absorb the full horror of what she'd witnessed in the shed. When she'd glanced at the breeding dogs and their puppies, her instinctive reaction had been to look away. She knew awful things happened in the world, of course she did. But it was different knowing something abstractly to being confronted by it in the flesh. It was the sadness in their eyes that had got to her, and it was only now, while she stood around giving Carly and Gemma time to escape, that the full horror was starting to sink in.

Deciding she'd given enough time for them to get to cover, she summoned all her dramatic training and sauntered over to where overalls man stood.

'Hello,' she said. He threw his cigarette butt onto the gravel and made to go indoors again.

'I'm so sorry, but I'm afraid I won't be able to purchase a puppy today.'

'What?' He went red in the face and glowered at her.

She swallowed her fear. 'I only came to view them. My husband is the one with the necessary funds, remember I told you? Um … but I do know someone else is coming to look at the puppies soon, so …' She backed towards her car.

'Someone else?'

'Oh, yes. Didn't you know?' She unlocked the car and got in. 'I'm sure they'll be here in a minute.' She started the engine and saw a BMW driving towards them.

'That'll be them now!' said Suzanne through the open window. 'Bye.'

She drove off at what she hoped was a normal speed. The breeze from the open window was welcome on her sweating face.

Eight

Gemma and Carly got back to the lock-up first. The recent events were still buzzing inside them, and as adrenaline left their bodies, Carly experienced some shakes but no spasming. Gemma kept a cool exterior, feeling more ready than ever to take the investigation further. During the ride back in the car, they had had a slightly hysterical chat about what would have happened if they'd been caught. Then they had talked about how they should proceed and whether Suzanne would be a good fit for the team. This last discussion was still going on when they entered the lock-up to find Mary gently snoozing, knitting slumped in her lap. She woke with a start when Gemma banged the door behind them.

'Oh, they've been good as gold,' she said, smiling at Gemma's grimace. 'Too good it seems. I must've dozed off. Oh well.' She gathered up her knitting. 'I'm glad to see you two are all right.' She struggled to her feet and stretched. 'Is the new girl not with you?'

'She's not the new girl,' said Gemma.

'You said she was the new girl when we were locked in that storeroom,' said Carly.

Gemma felt her irritation rising. 'I just couldn't remember her name.'

'Well,' said Mary, 'I shouldn't hear too much of this.

The less I know …'

'Quite,' said Carly. She unlocked a drawer and handed over a few notes. Mary didn't count the money. She simply slipped it into her bag with her knitting and doffed an imaginary cap at them as she left.

'So, what you're saying,' said Carly, once Mary's candy floss head had disappeared, 'is that Suzanne wouldn't be as much of a help to us as Mary is.' She jerked her thumb towards the door.

'Mary doesn't really know anything about what we do. Plus, this Suzanne girl hasn't proved herself. She's an unknown quantity.'

'Hasn't proved herself?' Carly was indignant. 'She just broke us out of a locked storeroom, on an illegal puppy farm, probably used by gangsters who arrange dog fights, definitely guarded by a massive bloke who could've overpowered any of us, and not only that, she covered her tracks too! Plus, she did it pretty much without question.'

Gemma shifted from foot to foot. 'Okay, firstly,' she said, counting off on her fingers, 'we don't know that she covered her tracks. Secondly, she didn't know about the gangsters. And thirdly, we, well, we just don't know … maybe we want someone who asks questions.'

'Seriously, that's the best you can come up with?' Carly sank down into the huge armchair and let it envelop her while she rubbed her aching leg muscles.

Gemma knew that the run back to the car had taken its toll on Carly. They had been so paranoid about being seen that they'd both half-crouched almost all of the way. Once they got to the car, Gemma had noticed Carly getting the shakes so had offered to drive. Her offer had been met with a grateful nod. Gemma looked at her friend now, knowing she was stupid to argue with Carly. Suzanne had acted very confidently at the puppy farm, that much Gemma had to admit. It had just been so long since she'd fully trusted anyone apart from Carly that it seemed strange to be considering welcoming a new person into their lives. If they brought Suzanne in, she'd have to be told everything, and Gemma wasn't sure she was ready to give up all that information just yet. She knew deep down that Carly was right, that they could do so much more for the animals if they got more help, but people were complicated. She would have to suss out Suzanne fast, because it was clear Carly had already made up her mind.

***

They heard a car draw up and stopped their conversation. Suzanne entered the lock-up. Nobody really knew what to say at first. The urgency of rescue had negated the need for pleasantries earlier, but now, in the silence of the lock-up, the atmosphere was a tad awkward. Carly broke the silence.

'Thank you so much for helping us. We really appreciate it.'

'I was glad to help,' said Suzanne. There was another silence. So many questions hung in the air, but nobody wanted to be the first to acknowledge them.

'Come and sit down,' said Carly. She patted the couch next to her armchair. Suzanne sat and Carly continued, 'So ... we don't normally get into scrapes like that'—Gemma raised her eyebrows at this but said nothing—'it's just we had to investigate that place without being seen, and the not being seen part was pretty important, so thanks again. You were fantastic.'

'That's okay.' Suzanne was hesitant. She had a haunted look about her. 'That place looked ... just horrible. I love dogs, and I had no idea there were places like that. Are there many?' She looked almost frightened to hear the answer.

'There are loads,' said Gemma. 'It's bad enough here in Scotland, but there are even more down south, mainly in Yorkshire. The really big centres for puppy farming are in Wales and Ireland though. And of course, that's not to mention the rest of Europe.'

Suzanne visibly slumped. She eventually shook her head and said, 'But Britain's animal welfare—'

'Is the best in the world!' Gemma and Carly chorused together.

'I've always looked at it like this. If it was babies being tortured, for example,' said Gemma, ignoring the eye rolling from Carly, 'and you know, it was legal'—Suzanne raised her eyebrows—'and Britain was the country where they were tortured the least, it wouldn't make it right, would it? It wouldn't make it moral.'

'Okay, I think we're wandering from the point a bit here,' said Carly.

'It's exactly the point!' said Gemma, folding her arms. She thought of all the farmed animals confined in tiny spaces for their whole lives then transported in trucks, crammed in, gasping for air, only to be unloaded and face a terrifying death at the other end.

'Okay, Suzanne,' said Carly, 'you may think we're a bit crazy ...' She waited for a contradictory statement but none came. She continued, 'But we feel that animals get treated abysmally in this country, and we try to do something about it. The way we do things can be a bit ... unconventional at times. The dogs in that place were

66

miserable, yes, but I think what Gemma was trying to say before was that, well, when you make it okay to buy and sell animals for money, anything goes.'

'But it's illegal. It must be!' said Suzanne.

'Well, some of it is, some of it isn't,' said Carly. She could see Gemma getting ready to burst into another tirade, so she spoke quickly. 'Basically, commodifying animals leaves them open to abuse, legal or illegal.' There was a pause while Suzanne digested this. 'Even if puppy breeding was kept to the legal level, it would still be cruel,' said Carly gently. 'The law isn't always moral. Just think of the suffragettes, the civil rights movement and all the times in the past that the law has let us down. Sadly, animals are the ones being let down by the law in this case, so we have to help them, because they can't help themselves.'

Carly handed her phone to Gemma, who had her own phone out, ready to see what evidence they'd got. 'Let's take a look at the video and photos, see if they turned out okay in the low light,' said Gemma. In no time, they were looking at the images on Carly's large computer screen. For the first time, Suzanne saw the place she'd just escaped from in detail. The audio didn't really do justice to the desperate cries that she'd heard in there. The smell wasn't represented either – that putrid odour of stale urine and faeces. But the images still delivered a punch to the gut that she hadn't been fully prepared for.

Some of the puppies were in cages. She hadn't noticed that at the time. They were grouped into different breeds. Pugs in one, cockapoos in another, huddled together from fear more than cold. Their shaking was highlighted in the spotlight from Gemma's phone as the recording moved from one cage to the next. There was a mother lying in sodden newspaper, because there was nowhere else to lie, her teats distended and filthy. One puppy suckled in a lacklustre fashion while she gazed into space, seeing nothing but misery before her. Other puppies who were not caged rushed up to the dividing fence, so hungry were they for any sort of love or affection. Suzanne could feel tears forming in her eyes.

'I didn't get as much footage as I'd have liked to,' said Gemma. 'Did get quite a few pictures though.'

The images flashed up on the screen, starting with the most distressing – the dead puppies in the bucket. Suzanne gasped and put her hand to her mouth.

Carly explained. 'Many of the puppies don't make it, so they just throw them away like rubbish. We saw that guy you met dump them up at the back of the property just before we got locked in the storeroom. They make enough money from those that survive to not care much about those that don't. This lot were transported in a trug in the footwell of an Audi, probably brought from one of their other bases of operations. Mind you, the puppies that survive long enough to be sold often don't last much longer than that, mainly due to the conditions they've been forced to endure. Disease is rife in these places.'

Suzanne bit her lip hard to stop from breaking down in front of these people she barely knew. The pictures kept coming – the crowded conditions, the tiny, miserable-looking puppies with weeping eyes and matted fur. Then came some shots of the Westies at the front.

Carly anticipated the question in Suzanne's rapidly reddening eyes. 'They clean these ones up, so they're presentable to potential buyers. They often try to rush people into a purchase before the buyers realise anything's wrong. Did the guy try to hurry you into buying a puppy?'

Suzanne nodded silently. Gemma continued to scroll through the pictures. They painted a pretty bleak picture of animal welfare in the UK.

Gemma said, 'We'll copy this little lot and get it all to the SSPCA, the League, One Kind and, of course, the police. Nothing much will happen, the laws just aren't there to protect these dogs, but it will raise awareness. We'll send it to the *Guardian* and the *Daily Mirror* as well. They're normally quite keen to cover animal stories.'

Suzanne looked at the little French bulldog puppies in the lock-up. Their comfortable playpen seemed like such a haven of happiness compared to what she'd just witnessed. It all seemed so surreal.

Carly saw her looking. 'We think those guys came from there. We ... acquired them to save them from a life of misery. Benji's given them all the once over. They're fine apart from one little guy who's got a heart problem. Benji's going to see what he can do. The others at his surgery don't know where his extra cases come from. They think it's charity work, which I suppose it is really.'

Suzanne wandered over to the puppies and finally spoke. 'I can't quite believe what I did back there. I lied to some massive guy about wanting to buy a puppy. I stole his keys from his office. I let you two out of that storeroom, put the keys back then escaped discovery by the skin of my teeth – all for people I barely know.' She took a deep breath. 'But I did it, because deep down, I knew it was the right thing to do.'

'You did good,' said Gemma, in spite of herself.

'It may seem strange,' said Carly, 'and it *is* strange, but what you did was absolutely the right thing to do.

69

Listen, we would love you to help us again in the future. You've shown that you're brave and resourceful, and you obviously care deeply for animals. Would you consider working for us part time?'

Gemma said hurriedly, 'We'd have to vet you, of course. And you'd be sworn to absolute secrecy.'

'But we would pay you a good rate,' said Carly, giving Gemma a sidelong glance.

Suzanne looked at the puppies then at Carly's expectant face and Gemma's slightly hostile one. The lock-up door clanged, and everyone looked over. It was Benji and John. Benji kissed Carly hello and looked troubled to see Suzanne's face so serious.

'Is everything okay, guys?' he said. The only sound was John's claws tapping against the floor as he trotted across the lock-up to be fussed over by Suzanne. 'Only Rose said you were trying to get hold of me at the surgery.' He didn't wait for an answer. 'Oh, and on that note, I'm afraid I have bad news.'

'What?' said Carly.

'I'm afraid the little fella didn't make it.'

Gemma walked over to the puppies and slumped beside them. Suzanne hugged John, and Carly hugged Benji.

'His little heart was just too weak,' said Benji, holding Carly to him. 'I did everything I could. That was the surgery I was in when you called. Poor little guy didn't even have a name.'

'Can I name him?' squeaked Suzanne. They all looked at her in surprise. 'I'd like to name him Chance, because you all took a chance on him, and I met a lovely dog called that just recently.'

'That's a good name,' said Gemma.

'Farewell, Chance,' said Carly, and Suzanne burst into tears.

'What has been going on here?' Benji asked Carly quietly.

'Later babe,' she said. 'Just the usual drama.'

Benji looked sceptical. 'What kind of drama?'

'It's maybe not the right time,' she said, gesturing towards Suzanne.

'What have you done to her?'

'I think we may have inducted her into the team.'

Benji looked surprised. Carly pulled him down onto the armchair beside her, hugging his waist. 'Oh, and babe,' she said, 'later on, when I do tell you everything that happened ...'

'Uh-huh ...'

'Promise you won't get upset?'

Thursday.

Things seemed even duller than usual in the jewellers' shop. There was precisely no one to talk to. There were no customers, and the manager was in the break room at the back reading *Grazia*. Suzanne unlocked one of the window cabinets and took out a tray of necklaces. She peered out into the shopping centre. It seemed quiet too. Locking the cabinet, she laid the necklaces on the counter, picked up a cleaning cloth and began polishing each one in turn.

The first one was a heart-shaped locket. The only people who ever bought these were grandmothers. They'd come in and know exactly what they wanted. It was normally for an eighteenth birthday gift or perhaps for a holy communion. Suzanne always thought the heart-shaped lockets were odd because photos never fitted into them very well. The dip of the heart usually cut into the middle of someone's face. She wondered whose face she'd put in a locket. Not being in a relationship or having any children, she supposed it would have to be a photo of her parents. *A bit sad at twenty-three,* she thought.

She moved from polishing the heart shape to running the cloth up and down the chain it hung on. Placing it back onto the tray and picking up the next necklace, a big, clumsy, round locket, she considered her position at the jewellery shop. The pay was rubbish, but then she could be working somewhere far worse for the same remuneration – somewhere she wouldn't have time to think about her life. She just felt so pointless. College had been great though maybe a bit of a waste of time? She'd enjoyed it, but her dreams seemed unrealistic now she was living in the real world. Nobody needed a performing arts degree. There were no real jobs in acting or dancing or singing or playing the cello. Who was she kidding? She was competent at them all but master of none. So here she was, polishing lockets for nobody to buy, for minimum wage.

Her thoughts wandered to the previous day. She'd never felt so nervous, so scared, so alive. Rocking up to that puppy farm was one of the craziest things she'd ever done. She had felt truly needed for the first time in her life. Without her, they wouldn't have got out of there. Without her, they couldn't have covered their tracks. Without her, the whole thing would have ended in chaos. And possible violence. She didn't like to think of that part, but at the same time, she knew that danger had to be part of a job like that. The puppy farmers were working in an unregulated, criminal world. They only cared for money and used living, breathing animals to get it.

She admired Gemma and Carly for breaking the law to get justice. Was that wrong? Was that utterly mad? She was amazed that Benji was involved in such a risky outfit. He'd always seemed so solid and calm and measured. Maybe Carly had talked him into it. *I bet that's what happened,* she thought. She replaced the big, ugly locket and extracted a small oval one. Carly and Gemma seemed so cool, so tough. And yet, they wanted her to help them. Her, a mediocre drama student from Newington. Well, her dramatic skills had certainly come in useful when breaking Carly and Gemma out. Perhaps her degree could be put to use after all. *There's no way I would ever have imagined using my acting skills to lie to criminals,* she thought.

She did have a steady job here though, and although the pay wasn't great, she could at least afford to pay her parents some rent and go out with her friends once in a while. *Mind you, they did say they'd pay me well,* she thought. *Surely, that means better than this place, but at what risk?* All she was doing at the jewellery shop was polishing things that hardly anybody bought, gift-wrapping the things they did and smiling vaguely at customers. If she worked for Carly and Gemma, she'd have more money and would be making a real difference. Maybe she could do both?

She picked out the next necklace and rubbed at it distractedly. Someone came in to browse. She said, 'Can I help you?' and they swiftly left. British sensibilities didn't allow for intrusive customer service. She'd obviously interrupted the customer's thoughts. *Well, she was interrupting mine,* thought Suzanne. She was onto her fifth necklace when the manager, Pam, stepped onto the shop floor. She had some biscuit crumbs on her bosom, but Suzanne didn't say anything.

'I'm just going to get some lunch,' said Pam, sweeping past her. 'I won't be long.'

'No problem,' said Suzanne to the empty space that Pam had left behind.

Perhaps, I could just look after the puppies they bring in, thought Suzanne, moving onto the sixth and final necklace on the tray. She had enjoyed fooling that giant of a guy in the overalls though. That sort of thing, she could do. She could outsmart people. Her brain was going slightly mushy being stuck in the shop day in, day out. Pleased with her polishing work, she straightened up the necklaces and put them back in the window. Locking the cabinet, she went for a stroll around the tiny shop to stretch her legs. She knew her fitness was dipping being here so much, but she couldn't afford a gym membership now that she didn't get a student discount. Maybe it was time to save up for a bike. Walking to and from work was hardly adequate exercise. She was just looking up how much bikes cost on her phone when Pam breezed back in. Suzanne hid her phone under the counter. Pam was clutching a sandwich, a packet of crisps and a can of Coke. Shoving the Coke under one arm, she punched in the code for the door to the break room.

Over her shoulder, she said, 'If you're looking for something to do, some of the necklaces could do with a polish.'

Suzanne waited until Pam was safely behind the door before sighing heavily. She stretched her arms behind her, making her back crack. *Okay,* she thought, *it's either this steady job with low pay where I'm literally bored*

stiff, help no one and have no control or ... or what?
Unpredictability, adventure, physicality, more money,
definitely helping people and using my initiative.
Spending time with adorable puppies and rehabilitating
abused animals were the ingredients for so many people's
idea of a dream job. However, a dose of criminality and
possible violence were not. *How bad can it be if Benji is*
involved? she thought. As she took another tray from the
window cabinet and picked up her polishing cloth, she
found herself thinking, *I could do with some danger in*
my life, I really could.

Nine

'She's too emotional,' said Gemma.

'We need someone who feels for the animals,' replied Carly.

They were strolling around the waste ground near the docks that they'd heard described by the men at the puppy farm. They'd found nothing sinister – so far. It was quiet, apart from the odd squawk from a seagull and the very faint distant rumble of traffic. A series of alleyways backed on to the derelict patch of ground, the high buildings blocking out noise from the city.

Thanks to the weakening effect of the previous day's shenanigans, Carly was on her crutches. Gemma kept pace with Carly, looking around every so often to check they weren't being watched. She knew that her friend wasn't really up to fieldwork. Carly had always tried to keep up with Gemma when they were kids but she was clumsy, or at least, that's what the doctors had said to begin with. The young Carly had dealt with the physical pain so well, a trait Gemma continued to admire her for. Eventually, it became apparent that Carly's muscles weren't developing correctly, and she had to be given special consideration at school. That was around the time that Duke had gone missing, and the two girls had leaned on each other heavily for mutual support. Gemma would go to Carly's house to cry, for although her parents were great, she hadn't wanted to appear weak in front of them. She had felt like a freak for grieving for so long, but Carly had understood.

Gemma would stand up for Carly at school when the other kids called her a spastic. It had been the catalyst for the development of Gemma's aggressive streak. If she punched a kid for bullying, she was the one who'd end up in detention, so she developed sneakier tactics. She learned to pick pockets, practising on Carly first then on her unsuspecting parents. She never stole from them, just tested herself to see what she could get away with. If caught out, she'd simply say she had been picking a thread from their trousers or go in for a hug. Slowly, she became an expert, stealing items from bullies without them noticing. Sometimes it even caused fights among the bullies themselves as they were a suspicious bunch, like gangsters who could never quite trust each other. Gemma would observe the chaos from the sidelines while fingering their lunch money in her pocket. Later, she would pass the money on to the bully's victims anonymously.

Carly had done her best to disapprove, but she couldn't put her heart into chastising Gemma when all she was doing was seeking justice. Gemma often thought that all she'd been doing since she was twelve years old was seeking justice – for Carly, for Duke and now for the terrified animals that were being exploited by cruel men. Since her parents' death, she had felt the need to fight for fairness and moral justice even more strongly. The need to redress the balance never went away. Justice had to be done, even if she had to do it alone.

They wandered on and came across a huge, modified

shipping container. It was rusty, though there was some meagre evidence that it used to be green. At some point it had been converted into something, but it wasn't quite clear what. With a glance around, they strolled round its large exterior, looking for evidence. They arrived back at the entrance and examined its door, finding that it was bolted shut with a heavy-duty padlock. They listened. Gemma banged on the door. The noise made Carly jump.

'What are you doing?' said Carly.

'Seeing if there's anyone in,' said Gemma.

'Who do you expect to answer the door with it bolted from the outside?'

'Not people. Dogs.'

They listened again but heard no barking. Gemma wandered off, and Carly stayed by the container, poking about with her crutches for clues. Soon returning with a couple of cracked milk crates, Gemma dropped one on the ground horizontally and balanced the other one on top vertically.

'I am so not saving you if you fall,' said Carly.

Gemma climbed on top of the precariously balanced milk crates, steadying herself against the wall of the container, and strained to see in through the high, small windows. She couldn't quite reach high enough. As she strained, she felt the milk crates wobble beneath her. They fell, and she jumped down, taking all the impact through expertly bent knees.

'There are spots of blood here, just by the door,' said Carly, pointing to the rough ground.

'This is definitely the place,' said Gemma. 'I just need to get up to those windows. See what they've got in there.'

She wandered off again. This time, she came back

with a discarded pallet. She dragged it under the windows and balanced the milk crates on top of it.

'I can't watch,' said Carly, watching anyway.

Climbing up was a slightly trickier business this time. Carly came over and held up one of her crutches so Gemma could steady herself against it while she straightened up. Now the windows were reachable. She gripped their minimal sills and peered in. Looking down, she saw what she feared she would. There were no dogs kept on site, but there was a bloodstained, carpeted floor surrounded by a waist-high wooden fence. At one end, there was a gate, while there was space for spectators all around. Otherwise, the container appeared to be empty, save for a few square, flat pieces of wood.

Gemma jumped down from her position in two stages and landed like a gymnast who'd slightly misjudged their landing. She brushed her hands together to get the dirt off and turned to face Carly.

'There's a fighting pit in there.'

Carly bowed her head, showing respect for all the dogs who'd been hurt inside the container's walls. 'Anything else?'

'Just a couple of boards that might be used to herd the dogs, but yeah, that's it. I couldn't get a photo, so we'll have to come back.' Carly looked unsure. Gemma spoke again. 'Well, I'll have to come back. We have to catch them in the act. This evidence is all very well, but if we don't manage to film it actually happening, we'll just get ignored.'

They began to make their way back.

'Do you know what I reckon?' said Carly.

'What?' said Gemma.

'I reckon you should come back. Not with me

though. Benji was unhappy about me coming with you today, never mind when there's a freaking dog fight going on.'

'So, I'll come alone.'

'No. What if something happens to you?'

'I can take care of myself.'

'I know you can, but what if Suzanne—'

'I'm not taking her with me!' said Gemma.

'Why not?'

'She's over emotional, completely inexperienced, and I'm not much of a babysitter.'

'Listen, mate, she's all we've got. Use her. Even if it's just as a lookout. She's fed up with treading water in life. Benji told me she really felt like she'd made a difference when she helped us out the other day ... once she'd got over the experience that is.'

Gemma looked annoyed while they walked in silence. Then a thought hit her. Looking triumphant, she said, 'She can't come with me. They've seen her. Mikey from the puppy farm will probably be at the meet, and he'll recognise her.' She folded her arms and gave Carly a victorious look.

'Yes, well,' said Carly, 'I've had a thought about that.'

Friday.

'You can't be serious.'

'I am serious.' Carly dangled the short, black, bobbed wig in front of Gemma. Benji looked on, clearly amused.

'Where did you get it anyway?' said Gemma. They were back in the lock-up, and Gemma was feeling a bit outnumbered.

'My sister was in a production of *Chicago* last year. She still has the outfit, including this wig,' said Benji.

'Well, your family are very bloody helpful, aren't they?' muttered Gemma.

Benji ignored her. 'I'm sure it'll be just the job for concealing Suzanne's long blonde hair.'

Just the job – what a typically Benji phrase to use, thought Gemma. *Urgh.* 'And what does Suzanne think of all this?'

'We haven't asked her yet, not specifically about this mission anyway,' said Carly. 'We wanted to get your approval first.' She and Benji both looked at Gemma solemnly.

Gemma knew they were trying to get her to see that they respected her. Maybe they did respect her, but it didn't change the fact that she only wanted to work alone or with Carly. This was going to be a tough and ugly undercover job. Although Gemma had seen dog fights online, she'd never actually been to one before. She could not prepare for the smell of the place or for being in among men who were baying for blood. The atmosphere would be raw and brutal. For the first time in a long while, she was scared. She couldn't admit it to these two, of course, but whenever she thought about the horror of the upcoming dog fight her stomach sank and lurched then sank again. There had been so much heartbreak in her life already – what was she doing taking on more? She thought about the innocent victims, all those lives that depended on her toughening up, and she had her answer.

'How fit is she?' asked Gemma.

'Pretty fit, I think,' said Benji. 'I know she went to the gym a lot when she was a student. She did dancing to a pretty high level before she started at the shop.'

'Can she run?'

'We'll ask her,' said Carly. 'We'll make sure she's fit for the job, because I really don't want you doing this on your own, Gem.'

'She's only, what, twenty-three?'

'Yes, but she's an adult. She can make her own decisions. She's already told us she wants to help us, and I think she knows there might be an element of danger again. I trust her, and I trust you to help her and guide her. We really need another member of the team if we're to keep going. I can't ...' Carly broke off, and Benji put his arm around her.

Gemma broke the silence. 'Somebody needs to be the brains of this outfit.' She was pleased to see Carly smile.

'Okay, so as the brains, I'm saying we need info. We need evidence and footage, and we need to know how these guys operate. We can only get that by going in. I'm simply not physically able to ... and that's okay. You know I'd help if I could.'

'You are helping,' said Gemma. 'You're talking me round. I can't give up on Colin's wee dog, Bella. I can't give up on all the others who were stolen and whose mums and dads are worried about them. I see their faces at night, Carly.'

Gemma could picture them all in her mind. She had an excellent memory, which was sometimes a blessing, sometimes a curse. There had been twenty dogs taken from the Edinburgh area in the last month – some trainable for fighting, others clearly to be used for bait. There were some cats missing too, but it was always tougher to know with them. They could simply be trapped in the garage of a neighbour who'd gone on holiday, or they could be being used for bait too, in the early training stages. She had memorised the names and faces of all the dogs, and the cats too, in the hope of one day seeing them all again, alive and in the flesh. She needed help to achieve that. She acknowledged that now.

'So, you'll take Suzanne with you?'

'Yes. But she has to be all in. Understand?'

'Absolutely. Thanks, Gem.'

Gemma looked at Carly as she turned back to her computer. Her eyes moved to Benji, with his hand still on Carly's shoulder, and John, lying at Carly's feet. She felt a sudden stab within her. They were calm and loving, just like her parents had been. They were her family. She really shouldn't be such a dick to Benji. He cared for Carly so much. Sometimes, she just found it so hard to smooth out her own rough edges.

Carly was looking to see if she could find out anything about the dog fighting gang on the Dark Web, but so far, nothing. They needed that evidence, and they needed it soon, if they were going to stand any chance of saving little Bella and the others. Gemma got up and went over to feed the puppies. It was a welcome distraction.

Ten

Colin walked their usual route. He'd locked up the house, as usual, and he'd turned right out of the gate, as usual, however this walk was anything but usual. The streets seemed quiet. They normally strolled this route in the evenings together, when the sun was low in the sky and everyone was finished with work for the day. He'd taken a couple of days off work. This was the time of day when the dog walkers would normally take Bella out during the week. They would take the pack of eager dogs down to Cramond beach where they could all run and play and have fun. She was always so happy when she returned from these adventures. He would cuddle her and snuggle her in a towel to get the last bits of sand out of her fur. He saw the dog-walking van picking up little Jasper from along the street. They waved awkwardly.

He felt empty inside without Bella beside him. It was so strange to see everyone else just going along as normal like nothing was wrong. His colleagues had said they were sorry, but he knew what they were truly thinking – that she was just a dog. He walked along with his hands in his pockets, missing the feel of a lead in his hand. He rounded the corner and entered the park they always went to. By the entrance, near the little play park that was fenced off for kids, was an A4 piece of paper taped to a tree. Colin stopped to read it. There was a photograph of two Yorkshire terriers and above the photo it simply read: *Jilly and Mathilda.* Below the photograph was a short paragraph: *Our beloved girls were taken from our garden on Tuesday. We are going mad with worry. Please, if you have any information, contact us. There is a substantial reward.* There was a phone number printed in large characters at the bottom.

Colin understood their desperation. *Tuesday,* he thought, *that was when Bella was taken.* They must have been doing the rounds. He photographed the poster and sent it to the organisation that had contacted him. He had a gut feeling they'd be able to help.

He still wasn't sure why he trusted them so much. Without knowing any of their names, he'd met an anonymous young woman in a car park. She could have been anyone. He could have been mugged, kidnapped or worse. Before going to meet her, he'd considered the risks, but his mind kept coming back to the same thought – he wanted Bella back. His desperation to have her back was fuelled by love and the knowledge of how vulnerable she was. It would have been bad enough to think of her out there if she'd simply run away, but the thought of his sweet, trusting friend in the hands of potential dog fighters … He pushed the thought to the back of his mind to avoid breaking down in the middle of the park.

He was beginning to regret taking the time off work. Perhaps if he'd stayed busy, he wouldn't be feeling so empty and useless. He couldn't run the risk of crying in front of the children though. That would lose him the respect which was vital for teachers to have in school. He just hoped the woman's investigation was getting somewhere. Walking the route he always walked with

Bella came from a desperate hope that it was all a big mistake. He wanted to believe it was just a coincidence that his neighbour had seen a suspicious van in the area when Bella disappeared. Perhaps if he walked their usual route, he'd come across her, alone and scared, having hidden herself in someone's shed or maybe found somewhere to sleep in the little collection of trees at the far end of the park. He wandered down there now.

He passed a woman with a boxer and nodded a greeting. The children's play park was deserted, all the kids either at school or nursery. He walked on across the bare grass and imagined Bella was running around chasing her ball. Eventually, he arrived at the trees and tried to look in among them without appearing suspicious. He was always conscious of how it looked for a man in his forties to be walking alone in a park. That was part of the reason he was always so happy to have Bella with him. It stopped the mothers staring. Suddenly, a small black dog darted out from the trees. Colin's heart leapt, and he ran after the dog for a couple of steps before he realised it was a little terrier, not his beloved Bella.

'Bitsy! Come here, Bitsy!' shouted the owner, a lady in a tweed jacket. She eyed Colin warily and called her dog to her side with the promise of a tasty treat. They walked off briskly, and Colin was left feeling both crushingly disappointed and slightly humiliated. He trudged off, circling back towards his house. He passed no other dog walkers, just a lady with an empty pram, walking in the direction of the nursery. She was on her phone and didn't even notice him. He wondered if she just wasn't allowed to leave the pram at the nursery or if she'd forgotten her baby.

It began to rain, and he quickened his pace. He never

did this with Bella. In any weather, the way back from the park was for stopping and sniffing and keeping him waiting beside lamp posts and bins and the postbox. It was the wind down after all the energy expended running and chasing after her ball in the park. He would have given anything to have his walk home slowed by such delays today.

Soon, he was back on his street. He looked at his phone and saw that his message about the Yorkies had been read. They were obviously looking into it. He had to hold out hope. He turned left, opened his gate and put his key in the door. Closing it behind him, he took in the silence of the house. Against all logic and reason, he called out Bella's name. Getting no response, he let the pain inside him double him over. He slumped onto the hall floor and wept.

Saturday.

'Okay, let's go over it one more time.' Gemma was pacing around the lock-up, and nobody was in any doubt that she was the one in charge. She had the experience in the field, which essentially meant she was the only one who had locked people in cupboards and kicked anyone in the throat. Suzanne, kitted out in her non-specific clothing, dark wig and heavy make-up, was a far cry from the hippy-dippy blonde who'd turned up at the puppy farm only days before. She hung on Gemma's every word.

'We park on the corner, so we can escape in a hurry, in any direction, if we need to. We shed any empathy, sensitivity or feelings on entry.' She stared hard at Suzanne, who nodded repeatedly. 'We don't give them our names,' Gemma continued. 'Nobody ever gives their names at these things, so it won't seem unusual. We do, however, answer the code question, which is: Did you see the match last night? To which we reply …' She pointed at Suzanne.

'Partick Thistle won,' said Suzanne.

'Very good. It's hard to gauge how many people will be there, but they don't organise these shows for just a few, so we should be able to blend in at the back. It will be dark on the waste ground, but the light shining from the windows should lead us to them, though it'll be faint at first as it's a long way from the road.'

Suzanne put up her hand. Gemma nodded at her to speak. 'Why don't we park with the others near the shipping container? Wouldn't it be easier for a getaway?'

'We can't run the risk of getting blocked in and not being able to escape.'

Benji, who had been listening to all this with mounting horror on his face, gripped Carly's shoulders and looked even more relieved that she wasn't going.

'So, once we're in, we want to try to get as much information about these thugs as possible. We also want to get footage of the fight and, more importantly, the faces of those attending. I'll do that as it'll mean going in towards the fighting pit. Suzanne can film from the back. Remember, filming is strictly regulated in these places so do it covertly. They're committing a crime and don't want to get caught. They'll also be in an aggressive mood and won't need much of an excuse to turn that aggression on you.'

Suzanne swallowed hard. This was quite a change from the jewellery shop. She tried to imagine the situation she was going into. Carly had told her she'd discovered from her research that this specific group of sick people liked to watch a smaller dog getting mauled by a fighter in between bouts. This was unusual, even in dog fighting circles, and showed just how vicious this particular ring was. She focused her attention completely on Gemma.

'Lastly, we may attempt to free a few dogs. Now, unfortunately, fighting dogs are difficult to get out of a situation like that quietly. There will be multiple fighting dogs in cages at the meet. There will also, hopefully, be bait dogs, generally gentler breeds who will be terrified. They may be injured, and they may lash out, but we are unlikely to be seriously harmed by a bait dog. They are deliberately smaller and easier to handle than fight dogs. If Carly's research is right, they'll be kept in cages out of the way of the pit, which is good for us. Once we've got all the footage we can get, and I feel that the time is right, I will give the signal to you to leave. You will then wait by the bait dogs' cage, and we'll grab them and get out of there – quietly.' Gemma now stopped addressing the group and turned to Suzanne. 'If you want out, I understand, totally, but now's the time to say.'

Suzanne's heart thumped hard in her chest. She thought of the poor mother dogs who she'd seen at the puppy farm. She thought of how Gemma and Carly had described dog fighting. She knew that the bait dogs at the meet might get thrown to the fight dogs at any time to get them psyched up. She may even have to witness this happening. Her thoughts went to the grief-stricken man who'd had his dog stolen by thieves, and she knew it was the right thing to do. She was compelled to help the innocents who were being tortured by these men. But still, she was frightened. She looked at Gemma and thought of the story Benji had told her about Gemma's childhood friend, Duke, and saw the steely look in Gemma's eyes. She felt a new determination rise within her.

'I'm in,' she said.

***

Gemma and Suzanne made their way over the uneven waste ground. They could barely make out the tiny chinks of light in the distance, but they became clearer the closer they got. Sensible shoes had been non-negotiable, and Suzanne felt unusually sure-footed in her trainers which were quite a departure from her normal, less practical footwear. Gemma wore hiking shoes and sported a militaristic look. Her clothes were all black as usual. Suzanne wore well-worn blue jeans with a plain navy T-shirt and jacket. The wig itched a bit, but Carly had stuck it down and pinned it on very firmly.

Approaching the lights, they saw several vehicles. One of them was a large white van. Suzanne noticed that it had one of those stickers in the window with crossed out hedgehogs on it. She was about to point it out when Gemma said in a low, serious tone, 'Remember, we don't give a shit about these dogs, okay?'

'Okay.'

'Well, until we rescue a few of them.' Gemma gave Suzanne a manic grin.

They were met not far from the entrance by none other than Mikey McGregor, giant overalls man himself. He'd swapped overalls for jeans and his T-shirt revealed a few aggressive-looking tattoos. Knives seemed to be a central theme. He glanced at the two young women, assessing them, then dumbly asked the code question.

'Did you watch the match last night?'

'Partick Thistle won,' they answered in unison. Suzanne wondered if this would sound suspicious, but Mikey merely nodded and waved them through. Gemma even went so far as to pat his arm as they went in, a gesture that said they belonged. Suzanne supposed women were a rarity at these events but, obviously, not totally unheard of.

The moment they stepped into the shipping container, they were immediately aware of the noise, the aggressive atmosphere and the unfamiliar smells. The air was heavy with blood and sweat and fear. They couldn't see much from the entranceway. The shouts that came from mostly burly, shaven-headed men were directed at the fighting pit, which was right in the middle as Gemma had described. The spectators had their backs to them, and there were more than a few plumbers' cracks to be seen. Right beside the entrance were some small cages. These contained a little spaniel, two Yorkshire terriers and a small collie. They were cowering and shaking, and it was all Suzanne could do not to scoop them up right then and run out of the door. She knew she couldn't risk drawing attention to themselves, but she could allow a rush of hatred for these men to pulse through her. Inadvertently, looking mean was making her disguise more believable, and Gemma nodded at her in approval of the sudden scowl that had appeared on her face.

'Stay here,' said Gemma. 'I'll be back as soon as I can.' Suzanne watched Gemma disappear into the crowd of milling male bodies, moving in the direction of the pit.

Eleven

Gemma had her phone in her top pocket. It had been set to record video in the dark before they had gone in. She crossed her arms when she approached the crowd, to protect herself and to keep the camera as steady as she could. Squeezing her way through the sweating, shouting mob, moving towards the pit, she found she was short enough to go largely unnoticed but tall enough to see what was going on. She managed to position herself in a gap behind two front-row spectators where she hoped the camera would pick up the full horror. Her baseball cap was pulled down low, practically glued to her head. She had no intention of being noticed.

On the opposite side of the pit were the fighting dogs in cages. They were near the pit so they could see and, more importantly, smell what was happening. Her heart went out to them. Some were bashing themselves against the sides of their cages, others just looked into the middle distance, panting heavily. She turned her attention to the humans who were dealing with them. Sure enough, Greg from the Audi at the puppy farm was taking bets nearby, and Stan, his odious companion, was handling the dogs.

A large, white dog that looked to be some kind of bull breed was led into the pit by a weedy man. The crowd cheered. A black Staffie, slightly smaller than his opponent, was led in by Stan. It seemed all bets had been laid, and the fight was about to begin. The pit floor was old carpet to give the dogs' feet better traction. Gemma really didn't want to witness the fight. It would be a horrific spectacle, and she felt she was betraying the dogs by doing nothing to stop it. However, she knew she had to film some fighting – the more evidence she had, the more time these guys could get. There was chanting, and Gemma tried to concentrate on getting footage of the crowd. Several men were leaning over the fence, jeering and shouting.

Finally, the dogs were released. The weedy man's dog, the large white one, rushed at the other, taking hold of his opponent's ear. The black dog tried to snap back but the white dog was large and had had his ears cut off. The black dog's ear was starting to bleed, generating a guttural roar from the crowd. The white dog let go and almost instantly clamped his jaws on the black dog's neck instead. Larger and stronger, the white dog shook his smaller opponent until drops of blood splattered his white fur. Stan jabbed his dog with a stick to encourage him to fight back, but the poor boy was helpless. Like a rag doll, he slumped and rolled over, seemingly begging for mercy. Gemma decided she had enough footage to secure a conviction and did not want to witness the conclusion of this carnival of carnage. She managed to back out fairly easily. There were plenty behind her who surged forwards, desperate for a better view of these two innocent dogs being made to tear each other apart. As she emerged, she spotted Suzanne, still standing in the shadows near the bait dogs.

'Did you get it all?' she asked.

'Yup, but I'm going to try to get some from the other

side.' Gemma patted her top pocket, and all the colour drained from her face. Her pocket was empty.

Without explanation, she dived back into the crowd. There was no way she was leaving without that phone. She scrabbled about on the floor, between legs and moving feet. She went largely unnoticed, the men's attention still taken by the grotesquely one-sided fight that was going on in front of them. She shuddered to think what was happening to that poor black dog. She knew she'd retraced her steps exactly and was almost at the front again. Her heart thudded when she considered her phone might have been destroyed by stamping feet. Then she spotted it. It had got kicked away and now rested in a gap in the fence on the bloodied carpet. It was reachable, but she'd have to get right to the front and risk being noticed. With measured manoeuvres, still crouched down, she got to the front. She reached out slowly and could see between the posts that the black dog was now being dragged along by the white dog. Someone stood on her hand and she snatched it back. The pain was strong, but the adrenaline was stronger. Edging further towards the fence, her shoulder pressed against it, she grabbed the phone and shoved it in her trouser pocket where it was secure. She turned to go but hadn't managed to stand up before there was a massive surge forwards, and her arm got caught under someone's foot. The owner of the foot jumped. She didn't snatch her arm back in time, and they landed heavily on her forearm, breaking it.

Pain surged through Gemma in a sickening wave. She cried out in anguish, but nobody noticed amid the other primal sounds. All her energy was propelled into her legs. It was fight or flight, and she was in no shape for fighting. She dragged herself to her feet and determinedly shouldered her way back out of the crowd, folding her broken left arm against her body. She stumbled out towards a horrified Suzanne. Unbeknown to Gemma, she had blood on her hand and face too. She looked like a woman possessed.

'Get the dogs,' she said to Suzanne with a primal grunt.

Shaking, Suzanne unpinned the cages, looking to Gemma for guidance. Gemma just pointed to the Yorkies and said, 'One each,' and to the larger dogs, saying the same. Suzanne was confused by the way Gemma was holding her arm, but the dark look on her face ensured that Suzanne didn't dare argue. She placed a Yorkie in Gemma's right arm and put the slip lead over the head of the spaniel, handing it to Gemma. Taking a Yorkie herself and the collie, they made for the exit. The large roar that had come just before Gemma's reappearance was surely the indicator that a dog had been killed. It was this thought that filled her with hate and determination and purpose as she strode out of the container. They went around the far side so as not to encounter Mikey and made their way back towards the car.

'Are you okay?' said Suzanne, when they were out of earshot.

'Just walk,' said Gemma.

They walked fast. The further they went, the darker it got. The spaniel was trotting along well, despite her short legs. The collie managed more easily, and Gemma could feel the Yorkie's heart beating fast against her palm. The slip lead was also on her right wrist making it an awkward journey. They were halfway to the car when they heard a shout. Suzanne looked back. Mobile phone flashlights were moving chaotically around the entrance to the shipping container. The collie must have sensed Suzanne's concern. He barked and suddenly the lights focused in their direction. Then, chillingly, the lights began to move, chasing after them. Gemma told Suzanne to pick the car keys out of her left pocket. Suzanne obeyed immediately, having learned not to ask questions.

'Run,' said Gemma.

Suzanne began to run, and the collie kept up easily. Gemma ran too, the poor spaniel getting lifted off the ground with every step. The shouts of the men chasing them were becoming louder. The collie became excited. He crossed over in front of Suzanne, and she tripped, landing heavily on her side.

'Get up!' Gemma was still running towards the car. Suzanne had managed to hold onto the Yorkie who was a little dazed, but the collie's lead had slipped out of her hand.

'Open the car!' screamed Gemma.

'The collie's loose,' shouted Suzanne as she scrambled to her feet.

'Just open the car.'

Suzanne took the keys out of her pocket and clicked them towards the car. It unlocked. Gemma opened the back door with great pain, put the spaniel and Yorkie into the back seat, slammed the door shut and ran back towards Suzanne. She told Suzanne to put her Yorkie in the back seat.

'Can you drive?'

'Yes,' said Suzanne. 'But the collie ...?'

'I'll sort it,' said Gemma and ran back to the edge of the waste ground. The shouts and lights were dangerously close now, and Gemma was feeling dizzy. The pain was excruciating, but through it all, she summoned an image in her mind – an image of a collie who had been stolen on the other side of town from where Colin and Bella lived.

She called into the dark. 'Max! Maxxie! Come here, Max! Come on, Max!' She was sweating. She couldn't leave Max to these disgusting excuses for humanity who were pelting towards her. Suddenly, she spotted him.

'Max! Come here, boy! There's a good boy!'

Max came to her. She grabbed his lead with her good hand and belted towards the car.

'Start it!' she yelled.

Suzanne did so. The dogs in the back were barking with excitement. Suzanne opened the door for Gemma from the inside. Gemma leapt into the passenger seat and yelled 'Go!' Suzanne screeched away from the kerb, Gemma's door still swinging open. Gemma tensed her muscles to stop from falling out and held Max tightly on her knee. Once they were driving straight, Gemma managed to reach over and shut her door, and Max slid down into the footwell. He looked up at her expectantly. She was crying with pain.

Suzanne said, 'What happened to you?'

'Broke my fucking arm. We may need to stop in a bit so I can vomit, but just get us out of here for now.'

Suzanne was silent and focused on the road ahead. She gripped the steering wheel so hard her knuckles turned white. They were breaking every speed limit. Gemma looked into the back seat to see the spaniel and two Yorkies panting and yawning from stress. One of the Yorkies was trying to curl up to go to sleep in a desperate bid for calm after so much anxiety. She looked down at Max again, sitting between her feet. He was panting too, but his face was bright. She patted her lap. He jumped up onto it, and she hugged him to her with her good arm.

Burying her face in his fur, he absorbed her tears of pain and even licked them from her face every so often. They raced in the direction of the lock-up, and Gemma felt safer with every minute that went by. She continued to hug Max and even managed to smile when the car informed them that neither driver nor passenger was wearing a seatbelt.

***

Carly was already tapping away at her computer. Suzanne had made a very brief call from the car. Apparently, she was driving, having laid the phone down in the car and put it on speaker. Carly had asked why Gemma wasn't doing the driving. The question had been ignored. Instead, she was told by Gemma that they'd recovered four dogs. The collie named Max, the Yorkies named Jilly and Mathilda, and a spaniel called Raymond. A lousy-sounding Gemma also said there was no sign of Bella and could Benji get these other dogs back to their owners tonight.

So, Carly had contacted the owners on social media, all of them eagerly giving her their details. *Just as well I'm not a scammer,* thought Carly. She had had to field a lot of questions about who they were and where the dogs had been found. To each question, she answered with the same statement. 'We're a covert organisation that seeks justice for abused animals.' Carly asked if they'd be willing to talk to the police once the case had been investigated further. All happily said yes and were now sitting at home, waiting excitedly for the return of their pets. Some were suspicious. Had this organisation stolen the dogs in order to demand a reward? She assured them they'd be collecting no money. Could they be people who simply couldn't sell the dogs as they'd intended and had grown a conscience? Carly ignored this and gave them all instructions. They'd be informed of a location and time near their home shortly. Their dogs would be left there for pickup. Carly couldn't risk their car being seen. If anyone did report them, things could get complicated.

Carly wondered about getting in touch with Tess. Tess was Carly's contact at Police Scotland. A friend from early primary school, Tess and Carly had always kept in touch even after Tess' family had moved to Skye to open a bed and breakfast. The trust between them was implicit. At eighteen, Tess had moved back to Edinburgh to do police training and now worked at Fettes. She was a senior figure in the IT department and could access all sorts of records then cover her tracks. If an officer accessed information on the police network that seemed unusual, they'd be questioned and perhaps even disciplined, but Tess could beat the system as she pretty much was the system. Carly always got the impression that Tess still thought of Carly and Gemma as they had been when they were eight years old. They were the trio that had turned into a duo, and Tess hadn't witnessed the massive changes in the other two's lives when Carly's illness had progressed and Gemma's parents had died. Tess couldn't be linked to any animal rights organisations formally, but she'd always kept in touch with them secretly. On a par with Carly when it came to IT skills, she leaked them information even though she knew, if discovered, she could be fired. Carly and Gemma regarded her as a hero, but they knew others would not.

Carly located the nearest street cameras to each victim's home and hacked into the feeds. All was set for the safe return of the stolen dogs. Now she was searching for anything that would tell her where Bella and the other missing dogs were. She'd tried this search before, but sometimes an old search on a new day could bring different results. This was what she was working on when Suzanne staggered into the lock-up with Max and Raymond on the slip leads.

Carly took the leads from Suzanne who stumbled out again without a word. She returned with Jilly and Mathilda, one in each hand. Behind her, helped in by Benji, was Gemma, bloodied and deathly white. Carly closed the door once John had followed them in. She slipped the leads off Max and Raymond.

'I met them on the way in,' said Benji, gently lowering Gemma onto their couch.

'What the hell happened to you two?' Carly's brow furrowed. She guided Suzanne to an easy chair and gently prised the two little dogs from her hands. When released, they had a quick sniff around then settled next to John on his oversized cushion. Max and Raymond lay nearby, panting gently. Everyone seemed either exhausted or deeply concerned, apart from the puppies, whose squeaks and snuffles punctured the charged atmosphere. Benji knelt by Gemma.

'It's broken; we'll have to get you to A & E.'

'You fix it,' she said weakly, her mouth dry and speckled with dried vomit.

'I can't, Gemma. I'll give you something for the pain and something for the nausea.'

'They'll ask me questions,' wailed Gemma.

'It's Saturday,' said Carly; 'tell them you got stepped on in the mosh pit.'

'I did,' said Gemma with a mirthless laugh.

Benji gave Gemma painkillers and anti-nausea drugs before putting her arm in a splint. He then attended to the dogs. They were all thirsty and hungry, which was easily dealt with. Max had sores on his paws, probably due to being forced to stand in his own urine.

'I'll put a wee note on his collar,' said Benji, dabbing Max's paws gently with antiseptic. Max lay on his side, and when his nose caught the scent of the ointment, he raised his head and made to lick it off. Benji firmly but kindly laid his hand on Max's head till he was lying down calmly again then stroked his face and ears.

Carly had made Suzanne a cup of tea.

'Thank you,' said Suzanne and held it to her like a comfort blanket. 'I think it's all just beginning to hit me now,' she said, blowing on the tea.

'What did you see there? What happened?' asked Carly, having given up on Gemma who was lolling on the couch, eyes rolling.

'It was so awful, Carly. The atmosphere in there was … evil. I've never seen people behave like that. I mean, I just hid in a dark corner really, next to these guys.' She nodded at the four former bait dogs, who were currently tucking into hearty meals. 'It was Gemma who went all in. She was right in among them. I was amazed they didn't notice her, but now I think about it, there were several men, crouched down, shouting, straining to get closer to the … fighting pit, so I suppose one more jostling body wasn't that noticeable. Gemma got footage.'

Carly approached Gemma and extracted her phone from her bloody pocket. The screen was cracked, but the phone still looked to be intact. Gemma opened her eyes briefly and looked straight at Carly. 'Dogs' blood,' she said. Carly patted her head gently, and Gemma relaxed back down onto the sofa.

'Okay,' said Carly, 'let's see what we've got.'

'Do you mind if we don't,' said Suzanne, surprising herself with how strident she sounded. More softly, she said, 'Only, I think I've taken all the violence I can for tonight.'

'No problem,' said Carly, setting the phone down next to her computer. 'So, can you tell me anything about tonight that might be useful to us?'

'Well, the guy asking for the password was the same guy from the puppy farm – the big bloke in the overalls. I think I heard someone call him Mikey.'

Carly started taking notes and nodded at Suzanne to continue. 'So, then we got in, and to be honest, all the men in there looked the same. There were cages with these guys in'—she nodded at the dogs again, who had finished eating and were getting fussed over by Benji— 'and then, when I took a peek round the side of the crowd, I saw the cages at the other side which I assume contained the fighting dogs. Gemma told me in the car that the two men you saw from the Audi were there too. The one called Greg was taking bets, they had a chalkboard for doing that, and Stan took a dog into the ring. There was another slimmer man who also had a dog in the ring. That was when the fight started, and I just went back to the corner.'

'That's all the dogs ready to go,' said Benji. 'Suzanne, would you like to come with me to drop them off, then I can give you a lift home?'

'That would be great, Benji. Thanks.'

'I'll just let the owners know where to pick them up.'

Carly started typing again. 'I've sent the instructions to your phone, babe.'

'Okay,' said Benji, getting leads on the dogs, gathering and loading them into the car. Suzanne got up to go.

'So, how did Gemma break her arm?' said Carly.

'She lost her phone in the melee. When she reached in to get it off the floor somebody stepped on her arm.'

Carly sucked her breath in through narrow lips and changed the subject. 'Have you told me all you can think of? Did you see anything on your way out?'

'We were too busy running away from the men chasing us to notice much. They must've seen the dogs were missing. Then they heard Max bark and came after us. It was so scary, Carly. Gemma was amazing. I mean it. Amazing.'

Suzanne shrugged on her coat. 'Oh, there was one thing I noticed on the way in. It's probably nothing, but there was a white van parked there that had one of those horrible stickers on it—'

'With hedgehogs crossed out?' said Carly.

'Yes!' said Suzanne. 'How did you know?'

Twelve

Benji pulled his cap down low and slipped Raymond's lead around the lamppost. It was a slight jab to his soul when Raymond looked up at him, sensing abandonment. 'It'll only be for a few moments, boy,' whispered Benji.

Retreating round the corner, he stood, staring at his phone. Carly had streamed the security camera's feed to it, and before a minute had elapsed, Raymond's human mum and dad came striding along the street. It was dark, but they spotted Raymond straight away and rushed up to him. Benji's heart leapt as he witnessed the little spaniel's tail, and indeed his whole body, waggling with delight. Benji walked briskly towards the car. One down, three to go.

Suzanne left Jilly and Mathilda, the two Yorkies, with their leads tied around a bike rack on the neat little housing estate where their owners lived. She wondered if they were sisters. They watched her go as she pulled Benji's cap down to shield her face but then seemed to recognise their location and began to bark excitedly. Suzanne quickened her pace. When she reached the van, she saw Benji smiling, his face lit up by the light on his phone. 'They've just been picked up,' he said.

While they drove to Max's family's location, they talked about the bizarre evening.

'You did amazingly well tonight,' said Benji.

'Thanks, but I don't think I did much.'

'Nonsense, you managed to get Gemma back safely and, you know, cope with Gemma generally.' He smiled.

'What is the deal with her?' asked Suzanne. 'What drives her? I've never met anyone like her.'

'Well, I think those are maybe questions for the girls to answer. I'm part of things, but they run the show.'

'And where does she get the money to do these things and to live? Does she have a job?'

'Well, as I say I ... uh ...' Benji guided the car round a corner. They drove for a while in companionable silence. Suzanne scratched Max's ears and wondered if she'd been too forward with her questions. She didn't want to put Benji in an awkward position. But she wanted to know at least something about the people she was going to be working with, especially if they were to make a habit of going into dangerous situations together.

'Well, this is in the strictest confidence, even though I suppose I'm not telling you anything that's not public knowledge. Gemma's parents died when she was young,' said Benji eventually. 'I think she was seventeen or so. They left her ... well, they were very well off.'

'Oh my God, I had no idea. How did they die?'

'It was a car crash. Someone driving a high-performance BMW was overtaking recklessly on a country road. Hit them head-on. I'm pretty sure it was instant.' His voice lowered respectfully.

'That's dreadful.'

'I know. I have no idea how I would've coped with such a thing at that age, but it hit Gemma pretty hard, as you can imagine. She was almost unreachable emotionally for over a year, so Carly tells me. Then, at some point, a few years later, she decided to sell their house and invest the inheritance in high-interest accounts and the stock market and so on, so she could do this stuff. She lives really simply and just devotes her life to animals. She's very driven, as you say.'

'I suppose it must feel good to have a purpose in life,' said Suzanne, staring out of the window at the passing suburban streets.

'We're almost there,' said Benji.

He parked between houses in a dark spot, as incognito as one could be in suburban Edinburgh. Suzanne gave Max a quick cuddle before Benji took him out of the car. She watched them trot along innocently, as if just out for an evening walk. Max's health-advice note dangled from his collar. She sat in silence, watching them disappear around a corner. Scratching at her wig, she suddenly realised that she had been partly responsible for these dogs' safe return. Tonight, they'd be fussed over by family and loved and cared for instead of … she didn't like to think about that place. Some folk really did treat animals appallingly. Not everyone, of course, but some people were just so utterly callous and psychotic. It also seemed to Suzanne that the law didn't do too much to protect these vulnerable creatures. Gemma had told her that, even if caught, these evil men would get a few measly months in jail, and that was if they had a watertight case built against them. You could get five years inside for fly-tipping. Suzanne rubbed her face and came to the conclusion that the world was screwed up.

She spotted Benji returning. He was beaming. 'All safe and sound,' was all he said. He turned the car around, and they drove off in the direction of Suzanne's house. She freed herself from the wig while they drove and tossed it in the back seat. *The world may be screwed up,* she thought, *but these guys are fighting to put it right.*

Sunday.

Carly sat down to watch the footage. She'd put a blanket over Gemma, who was now snoozing with her splinted arm resting across her chest. It was early on Sunday morning, so she would take Gemma to the hospital when she woke up. The later they left it, the quieter A & E would be.

Images from the evening were a bit shaky and some were badly framed, but there was no doubt about what was going on. The noise of the place blew out the microphone on several occasions. When it came to the actual dog fight, the images were disturbingly clear. Carly tried to focus on the faces in the crowd to spare herself the pain of looking at two innocent dogs being coerced into ripping each other to pieces. At least Gemma had managed to get more than half the crowd on film for the police to pore over. Guys who attended these gatherings were often involved in other crimes, so the cops might get a few arrests out of it.

Carly looked again at the main players. Greg keeping score and Stan with the black dog, she recognised from the puppy farm. The slim guy with the white dog, however, also looked familiar. She called up a few of the sites she'd been looking at before for information. Scanning down a message board on the Dark Web, she found messages about tonight's fight. No, it wouldn't be there. Nobody would put their picture up and risk being discovered as someone who participated in dog fighting. There was a name in the discussion group that appeared to belong to someone who had been victorious the previous evening. That someone certainly wasn't shy about showing off about it. Nobby was his online name. He owned a white pit bull called Kaiser. The dog in the footage was a white pit bull.

Carly called up another site, known to be used by gangsters from Glasgow for a supposedly legitimate restaurant business. The greasy spoon was located in Govan. She knew it to be a front for laundering money. There was a picture of the establishment on the website, and Carly didn't find it too appetising. She scrolled down the page and there he was – the slim guy from the fight. The picture of him was even captioned: *Nobby*. He was listed as a 'dine and dash' which was code for something much more serious. It seemed he was in trouble with some pretty dangerous people. They never posted pictures of anyone on these sites unless they were an enemy. From the state of this website, she could see the gangsters weren't as tech savvy as her, but surely it was only a matter of time before they found him. She scrolled further down the page and noticed two new 'dine and dash' photos had been added since last time. When she saw the captioned photos of both Stan and Greg, she knew this was going to get messy.

She went back to the dog-fighting message board and kept coming across references to 'the group'. She could only assume this was some sort of group on WhatsApp or a similar encrypted messaging system that they used to share personal information that was too sensitive or specific to put on the internet. Carly spent a good hour going over the messages, trying to decode what it all meant and getting a feel for their communication style. She knew they could get to the bottom of this and find

Bella. She also knew time was against them as another dog fight had been arranged for next weekend. It was going to be a similar programme to the one they'd just had with bait dogs as a side show. However, Bella might be used in training before that and the next fight would be too late to rescue her. It was unlikely they'd use her straight away though, as they'd give the fighting dogs some time to rest.

Carly was still going over it all when Benji returned to the lock-up. He smiled at her and glanced over at the sleeping Gemma.

'How's the patient?'

'Oh fine, just kipping. I'll take her to A & E when she wakes up. I saw it went well with the dogs.' Carly indicated her multiple screens, three of which were still on the CCTV feeds.

'Yes,' said Benji.

'How's Suzanne coping with it all?'

'Okay, actually. She's pretty shaken up after tonight, but I reckon she's got real potential. It's just a case of persuading a certain someone to trust someone other than us.' Benji nodded towards Gemma. 'Anyway, what are you looking at here?'

Carly explained what she'd found and said they'd have to cook up a plan soon, or Bella would be no more – if she wasn't dead already.

'It's all so bloody grim,' said Benji, putting his arm around Carly.

'Yeah,' she replied, 'and all this information is meaningless if we can't access their encrypted group. That's where we'll find the specifics – times, locations, details of meetings, etc. It'll be too secure though. Not even the cops can get this information normally. That's why terrorists and guys like these use these encrypted messaging systems.'

'So, it all means nothing, unless we can access one of their phones?'

'Yes. And I mean physically access one of their phones. This is one of the few things I can't do remotely. But we don't have a physical phone.'

'Yes, we do.'

Carly and Benji turned around to see Gemma, still lying on the couch but with a phone held aloft. She was grinning maniacally again.

Thirteen

'How on earth did you get that?' asked Carly.

'Nicked it,' said Gemma, straightening up and looking surprisingly lucid compared to just a few hours before. 'I gave Mikey a friendly pat as we went in, and I nicked his phone.'

Carly leapt to her feet and almost landed on top of Gemma. She snatched the phone away from her. 'Wait, you did it on the way in? What if he'd discovered it was missing and came in after you?' Carly was looking at Gemma as a teacher would look at an unruly student.

'He didn't feel a thing,' said Gemma, waving away her concern.

Carly made her way back to the desk and swiped the phone screen while staring at the resulting display. 'Thank God,' she breathed, placing the flat of her hand on her chest as she sighed. 'They could've had a tracker on here. GPS would've given them our location in seconds. Gemma, you are the feckin' limit.'

Gemma smiled the smile of a drunk.

'Feeling better, are we?' said Benji.

'Yes thanks, doc. This splint has done wonders. I think I just needed a wee sleep.' Gemma got up and stretched her back. The look of despair from earlier in the night had gone and the colour was returning to her cheeks.

'We'll get you to A & E as soon as you're ready,' said Benji. He went over to check on the puppies.

Gemma sat down beside Carly and spoke in a low voice. 'I think it was just the shock of it all,' she said.

'What was?'

'All the wailing and the throwing up and the dramatics. I'm better now.'

'That's because Benji gave you drugs,' said Carly with a wry smile, reassured to see her friend back to her old self.

'Well, I know there's physical shock with breaking a bone, but honestly, Carly, the burst of adrenaline as we were escaping from those morons … I've never been in a situation like that before.'

'Yes, you have,' said Carly.

'But not with a broken arm and a sidekick who didn't know what the hell she was doing.' Gemma paused and clocked Carly's disapproving look. 'Okay, she did well. She did really well, actually. She just jumped into the driver's seat and floored it. I was … well, I was impressed.'

'No need to be so begrudging about it,' said Carly. 'Benji reckons she should become part of the team.'

'All the dogs back okay?'

'Yup. They're all cuddled up with their owners tonight. It's just such a shame there was no sign of Bella.'

'Yeah, I know.' Gemma's face fell. She pictured Colin's face when she had met with him. There could be no doubt that his dog meant the world to him. She'd do her utmost to make sure he got Bella back, broken arm or no broken arm. 'Any new info?'

'Well, yes, and now that we've got that phone, we

may actually get some useful intel.' Carly returned her attention to the phone, plugged it into a device attached to her computer and started tapping away at it. 'I can just see the basic functions right now, like the fact that location is switched off'—she looked pointedly at Gemma—'but the rest of it is password protected. It shouldn't take me too long to get in though.' Carly was eyes down now, and Gemma could see she was utterly focused.

'Right, doc,' she said to Benji, 'let's get this arm of mine in a stookie, so I can bash bad guys over the head with it.'

* * *

Gemma was utterly bored. After all the drama of yesterday, sitting in a hospital waiting room wasn't exactly thrilling. Carly was with her but was still looking at the phone. Benji had driven them there but was gone now as there was never anywhere to park. He'd pick them up later. She'd had her X-ray, and the doctors had ruled out surgery, so she was now waiting to get her arm put in plaster. The horrific dullness of Sunday morning television played away in a tinny fashion on a nearby TV. To Gemma, it was the soundtrack to empty lives, and she found it totally depressing. The chairs were comfortable enough but had the feel of those you'd find in an old folks' home, designed for awkward conversations and staring into the distance. Gemma let out a deep sigh.

Carly looked up from the phone. 'Do you know what I think?' she said. Gemma grunted in response. Carly continued, 'I think that Mikey is playing for both teams.'

Gemma raised her eyebrows.

'Not in that way,' said Carly. 'I mean that he

113

associates with both the puppy farming/dog fighting lot and also the Glaswegian gangsters.'

'Really?'

'Yes. Okay, Stan and Greg seem to be part of a Lothian based gang. They do business with Mikey and his parents, running puppy farms all over the eastern central belt. They also fight dogs as a hobby, and Mikey's obviously involved in that too, although I can't connect his parents to the fighting, not yet anyway.' She looked at Gemma to make sure she had her full attention. 'From what's on this phone, it seems Greg and Stan owe some gangsters in Glasgow *a lot* of money from a bet they lost on the dog fights. It says here that Stan and Greg and Mikey are due to have a meeting near Livingston in West Lothian on Wednesday, so I reckon if we get there first, we could have a chance of rescuing the other dogs. It seems pretty certain the location of the meeting is where they're kept. I've got the address and everything. It's an abandoned nightclub, and there's nothing to suggest they'll be there before Wednesday. They seem to be pretty busy with other dirty deeds.'

'That's all very well,' said Gemma, 'but with me laid up like this and you not in the best shape for carrying dogs, not to mention defending yourself against whoever might be there with the dogs, doesn't that leave us a bit stuck?'

'There's Suzanne.'

'They've seen her, once as herself and once in a wig. They're bound to try to find out who she is if they see her a third time, and if she wants to be part of the team—'

'So, you're willing to consider it?'

'As I said, *if* at some point in the future, she wants to be part of the team, she can't have her identity compromised.'

'Well, I can still drive,' said Carly.

They sat in silence for a while, the TV droning on and other patients' names being called.

'Why don't we just call the cops on them?' said Carly eventually.

'Because if they have strays in there, which they inevitably will, it'll just put more of a burden on the rescue centres, and I vowed never to do that. They're busy at this time of year with idiots dumping their dogs so they can go away on a summer holiday. We can find them homes, plus we know the ones who've been stolen, so we can just return them straight away. Also, the cops really have to catch them in the act doing something wrong. Sadly, stealing people's dogs doesn't count as wrong enough in our so-called civilised society. Maybe I should've called the cops once we knew where the dog fight was taking place. I don't know. All I know is, if they're caught with a few stolen dogs, they'll get a fine at most.'

'We'll send them the footage from the fight.'

'Yeah,' said Gemma, 'but again, if they're not caught in a more serious'—she made air quotes with her one good hand—'crime then they'll just get a slap on the wrist.'

'I reckon we need to set them up,' said Carly, looking at the phone. 'Mikey's obviously involved with both groups, so why don't we pit them against each other?'

'I like it,' said Gemma. 'There's no justice like gangster justice. We can't be implicated though, not even slightly. Those Govan guys are totally ruthless.'

'I reckon we get the dogs out then make Stan and Greg think the Glasgow guys took them. By the time they find out the truth, we'll be long gone.'

'It's dangerous but doable. We just have to find out who we'll have to deal with at the West Lothian location. I doubt that lot are there all the time. Maybe you could find out by sending fake messages on their WhatsApp groups?'

'Maybe,' Carly now looked unsure. It was all getting a bit real, the risks mounting.

'Well, whatever we do, we'll have to do it before Wednesday. We'll work it out together.' Gemma patted Carly's arm.

'Judith Payne?' The nurse called out to the waiting room.

Everyone remained seated until Carly nudged Gemma and mouthed, 'That's you.'

Gemma jumped up and strode towards the plastering room.

'This way, Judith,' said the nurse.

Gemma looked back at Carly and winked.

Fourteen

Monday.

They sat in a circle – Carly, Benji, Gemma, Suzanne and John. John liked to think he was very much part of the planning process. He was certainly a party to far more secrets than Mary ever was. He thumped his tail every now and again to prove he was paying attention, and Carly patted him whenever he did so.

'These are some very dangerous guys,' said Benji. 'Are we sure we want to do this?'

'This team's mission,' said Gemma, 'is to get justice for animals, justice they're not afforded by the law – yet. As I've explained, I think … well, we think'—she indicated Carly—'that calling the cops on these guys will only get them fines or suspended sentences or something equally inadequate. It's better to take the dogs from Stan and Greg's gaff, blame the Glaswegians using the phone we've obtained, then get out of there and let the villains sort it out. We reckon they'll probably deliver more justice than the law ever would, and the animals will be safely out of the picture. It seems, from the messages we've read, that relations between the two groups are at breaking point anyway, so it will just take a slight nudge to push them over the edge.'

117

'What about the puppies at the puppy farm?' said Suzanne.

Gemma rubbed her eyes. 'A problem for another day,' she said.

'But how can we be sure this justice, as you put it, will be delivered?' asked Benji.

'Look, Benji,' said Gemma, 'we can't be sure of anything. We're delving into an incredibly sketchy world. We will send the footage from the puppy farm on to the police and the footage from the dog fight too, so they will get investigated for those offences.' She turned to Suzanne. 'Sadly, even if we scooped up all the puppies and mothers from the puppy farms, they'd replace them with just as many within a few months. A full-blown rescue is just too impractical for a small team like ours. We know there are a limited number of fighting dogs and bait dogs to rescue, so we can cope with that, without burdening either the police or the rescue centres. Also, there's a chance that our plan will take these guys out of action, in which case their puppy farming business will be severely damaged.'

'Listen,' said Carly, 'it's not like we don't know it's a shot in the dark, but until the law improves, it seems like our only option to save Bella and any others being held with her.'

Suzanne glanced at the screens behind Carly. One of them showed a montage of dogs – all of them had been stolen to entertain a sick bunch of criminals. They all had families who missed them and desperately wanted them back. She thought of the joyful reunions she'd witnessed with Benji on Saturday night.

'So, what we thought was this,' continued Carly, 'Gemma and Suzanne will be in the van ready to take the dogs. I will act as lookout on the street. People don't tend to be wary of a wee woman on crutches.' There was a pause where Benji looked lovingly at his wife and Suzanne looked at her shoes. Carly went on. 'Benji's going to go in, get the dogs out and, hopefully, not meet with anyone as he does so. It seems the place near Livingston where they keep the dogs isn't occupied at all on a Monday or Tuesday, according to the messages, so we should be okay.'

'Who feeds the dogs then?' asked Suzanne. She was met with a full set of grim-looking faces. 'Oh,' she said.

'If you do run into anyone though,' said Gemma to Benji, 'I'll teach you all my moves for dealing with such an eventuality.' She grinned in that manic way of hers, and Benji made a face.

'How will we break in?' said Suzanne.

'Bolt cutters and a bit of knowhow,' said Gemma, tapping her finger to her temple. 'Right,' she said, hopping off her stool and adjusting her sling for comfort, 'let's be having you, Benji.'

Benji looked like he was about to be sick. Suzanne offered to be his sparring partner. They broke off into a group, Gemma demonstrating, among other things, how to take someone's legs from under them, how to defend themselves against a weapon and how to tie someone up quickly. Carly turned back to the computer, finalising details and seeing if there'd been any updates on the phone.

***

Carly had got up to stretch her muscles. Gemma had her stookie arm around Benji's neck, and they were walking through how to get out of a hold from behind.

119

Carly saw Benji's face and felt a pang. She didn't want to send him in alone, but what other option did they have? Now Gemma was explaining how they could clamp a weapon in their teeth or under an arm if they needed their hands free for something else. It was all getting a bit scary. They'd been at it for ages, and although Suzanne seemed to be picking up the moves well, approaching them like choreography, Benji still seemed unsure. Carly completed her walk around the garage and sat back down at the computer desk. She was still observing them when her burner phone rang. It was Colin.

'Guys, shut up!' she said, waiting for them to do so before answering it. They all stared at her. She gave them a meaningful look and nodded towards the phone.

'Hello?'

'Hello, it's Colin. I was contacted by you—'

'About Bella. Yes, we've been looking for her. Unfortunately, no luck yet, but we are trying.' Carly looked over to where they had been practising escaping from zip ties only minutes before and saw Gemma's ears prick up.

'Oh. Well, I just wondered if there's any way I could help. I know you're unofficial and everything, but I didn't get a chance to say to your colleague, as she ran off, that I really will do anything to get Bella back. She's … she's everything I have.'

Carly looked at Benji, who returned the look with his head slightly cocked to the side. 'You say you'd do anything?' said Carly. Gemma's eyebrows started to knit, and she shook her head. Carly spun around in her chair, so she was facing away from the rest of the team.

'Well,' said Carly, 'this might be asking too much, but …'

**

'You did what?' Gemma was beside herself.

'I asked him to help Benji on the mission,' said Carly.

'But you can't!' Gemma began to count off on her fingers. 'He's totally inexperienced, he's far too emotionally invested, he struck me as *very* straight-laced so who knows what his reaction to our methods might be, he might tell someone, he'd be useless in an emergency situation ...' She ran out of fingers so finished off by making a face at Carly and gesturing with her whole hand.

'Listen,' said Carly, unimpressed by Gemma's diatribe, 'all I'm saying is he can help Benji with the physical handling of the dogs, and if there's two of them, they can look out for each other. He sounded keen.'

'Of course he's keen! He wants to get his dog back. I'd be keen if I was him, but the fact remains that he has no idea what he's getting himself into.' Gemma began to pace.

'I think Carly's right,' said Benji.

'Well, of course you do,' said Gemma, scowling.

'Take it easy, Gemma. It's not just because she's my wife; it's because, well, I feel an enormous responsibility to these dogs and feel like ... what if I can't get them all out? I'm only one man, Gemma.'

'Yes, and that's another thing, why do we suddenly now need the help of men when we've been doing perfectly well with an all-female team up till now?' said Gemma.

'I've always been part of the team!' Benji was indignant.

'I know,' said Gemma. 'I didn't mean ...' She was

121

flapping her good arm around.

'The reason we need them,' said Carly, flaring her nostrils slightly, 'is because Suzanne is too recognisable, you've got a broken arm, Mary's an old lady and I'm a fucking cripple!'

Carly's words echoed and died in the huge lock-up. There was silence. Benji looked helpless, Gemma stared at the floor and John padded up to Carly, licking her hand tenderly. The hand was trembling slightly, but he continued to lick it until the trembling stopped. He then sat beside Carly, a calm and regal protector, daring anyone to hurt her.

It was Suzanne who broke the silence. 'It's probably not my place to say'—they all turned to look at her—'but I know I found that being emotionally invested wasn't a bad thing when I went to the puppy farm. I was totally inexperienced, but I think that caring can take you a long way.' She cleared her throat and continued. 'Obviously, the experience you all have is vital, but perhaps, you just need a couple of foot soldiers to help shoulder the burden of all this?'

She could see Gemma looking between Carly, Benji and herself, weighing things up. All eyes swivelled towards Gemma, and she finally spoke.

'Maybe I've been trying to do all this with just me and Carly for too long,' she said, sinking into the armchair. 'I'm the one in the field, and Carly's always been the brains.' She turned to Carly. 'I'm sorry if I haven't made you feel valued enough, because quite honestly, there would be no operation without you. I wouldn't know where to start doing what you do.' A silent understanding passed between them before Gemma turned to Benji. 'Of course, you've always been part of the team, Benji. Mending sick animals is an amazing skill to have, and I'm as grateful as they are.' He nodded at her in acknowledgement. She added, 'I'm sorry I'm such a dick to you.'

'S'alright,' said Benji. Carly squeezed his hand.

Suzanne felt wary as Gemma turned to her. 'I've been too quick to judge you, Suzanne.' Suzanne thought that was the first time Gemma had ever addressed her by her name. 'I think it's safe to say that you're part of the team now. Apart from anything else, you know too much.' This triggered quiet chuckles from all corners and lightened the atmosphere. John wagged his tail and went to Benji who ruffled his ears in cupped hands.

'So,' said Carly, 'we can bring Colin along?'

'I think he may be needed,' said Gemma, giving a deep sigh. 'Somebody's got to help out this tough guy.' She patted Benji's shoulder and he smiled. 'Ring Colin back with the details. We move tomorrow.'

Carly did so, and the plan to rescue Bella was in motion.

Fifteen

Tuesday.

Their van was as nondescript as it could be. It looked much the same as any work van that trundled builders' materials throughout the country every day – except this van was different. It was equipped with everything you might need for transporting dogs and keeping them comfortable on the journey. They had brought carriers lined with comfy blankets, water, food and the bowls to serve them in, slip leads, fully breathable muzzles, poop bags and towels in case of accidents and, of course, toys – nothing squeaky, just soft and comforting and quiet.

Gemma, Carly and Suzanne sat in the front, and Benji sat in the back out of sight. Mary was looking after John and the puppies. She'd promised not to fall asleep this time. If he was honest, Benji trusted John to be more responsible than Mary. Beside Benji was a very jittery Colin. He had worn dark clothes as instructed, but when they'd picked him up, Benji had noticed Gemma's sceptical look when the primary school teacher climbed into the van wearing black cords and a navy polo shirt. Benji too had his doubts. He was no macho man himself, but this guy made him feel like a muscled action hero. They'd barely talked on the journey as nerves were running high. However, Benji had taken the opportunity to remind Colin that they were just there to rescue the dogs and that was it. They were helping the victims of crime, and although breaking and entering might seem wrong, it was most definitely justified in this case.

They'd told Colin as little as possible, but if he wanted to turn them in, he had more than enough information to get them arrested. However, everyone felt that he was a man on a mission to save his dog and quite clearly had no other agenda. So much of what they did was based on trust, and even though trust didn't come easily to Gemma, she'd made a connection with Colin. They may not be confident in his abilities, but they had no doubt about his motives.

They came to a stop, and Gemma slid back the partition between the cab and the back of the van. 'Right,' she said, 'Carly's got the stuff to get you in. Once you're in, you just get the dogs out here to the van as quickly and quietly as possible. Colin, leave the fighting dogs to Benji – he can handle the muzzles if they're needed. You've got the leads there. Suzanne and I will be here to help get the dogs in the van. Carly will be on lookout and will ring Benji's phone if there's any sign of trouble. There shouldn't be. We know they leave this place empty on a Tuesday and the meeting's not till tomorrow, so no need for them to be here now.' She took a deep breath. '*If* you should run in to anyone, in the first instance, run. Just run back here. We'll have the doors open and be ready to go. It'll probably just be one guy, so Benji, if you're cornered, you know what to do.'

Gemma looked him straight in the eye, and he gave what he hoped was a convincing nod. The brief training Gemma had given him had been focused and clear. Now, though, thanks to the nerves of the day, he was struggling to stop it getting all confused in his mind. He just hoped he wouldn't need to use any of it.

They got out of the van. Carly, Benji and Colin made their way down the road and around a corner to the side entrance of the warehouse. It was beside an alleyway that was too narrow for the van to fit down. The building had been used for out-of-town raves in the nineties and now lay all but derelict. Gemma and Suzanne opened up the back of the van, ready to receive the dogs.

Carly used the bolt cutters on the padlock to the building, and it opened up easily after that. She went to her lookout post on the corner and left the boys to it. The exterior of the long-abandoned building was covered in several layers of dog-eared posters, so no windows were visible. Like the shipping container, the only light came from on high, in this case, from skylights.

The two guys spotted some dogs straight away. They all looked to be bull breeds, so Benji approached them first. The dogs were being kept in cages along one wall. Benji had mini bolt cutters with him in case any of the cages were locked. Colin suddenly ran towards them. Benji could see him desperately searching for Bella, but even on closer inspection, it was clear that these were just the fighting breeds. Benji took a muzzle off his arm and threw the rest on the floor. Approaching the first cage, he was watched closely by a Staffie while he fiddled with the cage door. The dog was suspicious but not aggressive. Benji spoke in hushed, reassuring tones which the Staffie responded to well. He slipped the muzzle on, and the dog put up no resistance.

'Lead please, Colin,' he said. Colin slipped a lead off his neck and handed it over. 'Right,' said Benji, 'you take

126

this one out to the van, and I'll be right behind you with the next one.' Colin took the lead reluctantly, still looking for Bella. He did as he was told though after an encouraging nod from Benji who had released another dog, a pit bull cross. They bundled them into the van, and Gemma and Suzanne made sure the dogs were comfortable. Soon after, they brought another two fighting dogs out to the van, both of whom had disturbing puncture wounds to their faces and front legs. As the dogs made their way to the van, they looked sad rather than aggressive. Benji wondered how that demeanour might change when it came time for him to apply stinging antiseptic to their wounds. There were just two remaining, and Colin was given the milder of them to take back to the van.

Benji could see the fear in the last dog's eyes. He too was wounded, and the cuts to his mouth and ears had not seen medical attention. They'd probably been left to fester for days. Benji undid the cage door and the dog lunged at him, barking ferociously. Closing the door quickly, he talked to the dog in hushed tones while it watched him with confused eyes. He suspected the poor beast had probably never been spoken to kindly. He took a treat from his pocket and gently offered it through the wire mesh. The dog growled and looked afraid even to sniff it. More gentle talking and the dog finally licked the treat from Benji's hand. If what the girls said was right, these dogs probably hadn't eaten for days. Gently undoing the door to the cage once more, Benji popped a treat inside a muzzle, and in a second, the dog had plunged his face in to get it. Benji expertly did up the muzzle, and they trotted to the van as though they'd been best pals for ages.

127

When Colin and Benji returned to the building, Colin looked stricken. They searched around for other dogs. The place was open plan, so there weren't many places to look. Benji was just working up to telling Colin they should probably go when they heard it. A bark, coming from a dark corner that harboured a cupboard they'd not noticed before.

'That's Bella!' yelled Colin and rushed up to the cupboard.

'Keep your voice down,' said Benji, running up to join him. Although they'd just rescued six fighting dogs, there had been relatively little barking. Benji didn't want to be discovered now through their own exuberance. Colin was pulling at the locked cupboard door like a man possessed. There was a padlock on it that was too big to be broken by the tools Benji had.

'Wait here,' he said to Colin, who needed no persuasion to do just that. Benji rushed out to Carly.

'All done?' she said.

'No, Bella's locked in, and I need those bolt cutters.' Carly slid them out from behind her back where she'd been hiding them. 'Thanks, babe,' he said, kissing her before taking them. He ran inside to join Colin.

'Stand aside,' said Benji, in his most authoritative voice. Colin had gone from nervous, reluctant participant to frantic, loose cannon, and Benji knew he had to be firm with him. He cut the padlock and took it off. Colin rushed to open the door. Inside the cupboard, there were six more cages. *Great,* thought Benji, *I hope we have room for this lot.* The cages were arranged with four at the front and two at the back. They looked like they'd been piled in with very little thought at all as the cages at the back were inaccessible. Colin attempted to dive over the front four to get to Bella who was in one of the back cages, along with a Border collie.

'We have to get these ones out first,' said Benji, undoing the latches on the front cages and slipping leads on the small dogs. They came willingly. Benji decided to take the first four out and leave Colin to get Bella and the collie. As he ran out with four leads, two in each hand, he heard Colin throwing the empty cages out of the cupboard with great force, so he could get to Bella. Benji ran to the van and told Gemma, Suzanne, and Carly when he ran back past her, that there were two dogs to go, one of whom was Bella. He expected to see Colin emerging victorious as he approached the door, but there was no sign of him. As Benji ran towards the cupboard, he saw the cages strewn on the floor and heard an anguished Colin saying over and over, 'Daddy's trying. Daddy will get you out.'

Benji said 'What's the problem?'

'The latches are broken, I can't get her out.' Bella was attempting to lick Colin through the wire.

Benji had to shove Colin aside to get a look. It seemed both cages had had their latches bent when the other cages had been hurled against them. He got out the mini bolt cutters and cut through the mangled latches easily. Bella was free, and Colin gathered her up in his arms with unbridled joy. She licked his face as if her life depended on it.

Benji freed the collie and said 'There'll be time for that later. Let's get out of here.' He slipped a lead over the collie's head and all four of them headed for the door. That's when Benji heard a noise that made his stomach flip.

His phone was ringing.

Sixteen

'That's the signal,' said Benji. Colin looked at him, but he was still caught up in the joy of being reunited with Bella. Benji fixed his eyes on the door and shouted, 'Run!'

Benji ran with the Border collie in tow. Colin soon got the idea and followed them at speed with Bella, who was now on a slip lead. They were almost at the door when their exit was blocked by three angry-looking men, one of whom was holding Carly roughly by the arm. One of her crutches dangled from the other arm, the second crutch was nowhere to be seen. She gave Benji an anguished look. Benji, Colin and the dogs stopped short, and the men slammed the door behind them. It bounced slightly, the latch not catching, but one of the men remained standing in front of it preventing anybody from leaving. The door blocker folded his arms and scowled. He was quite slim but had an intimidating look that said Don't Mess.

The guy who was holding Carly was wearing a pink shirt, a shiny suit and loafers. He also had a large bruise under his chin. The third man, slightly thicker set than the others, held a large, serrated knife which he pointed at Benji who had instinctively moved to protect Carly.

'Not so fast,' said knife man. 'Tie her up,' he said to

the man with the bruise who did as he was told, zip tying Carly's wrists and legs to a chair. Her crutch lay useless and out of reach, having been snatched from her and thrown away.

'And these lot,' said the man with the knife, 'get them tied up.' He pointed the knife towards the dogs then thrust it in the direction of Benji and Colin's faces. The guy with the bruise took the dogs and tied their leads to a pillar. Colin held on tight to Bella's lead, his knuckles white, as it was snatched at and then forcibly wrenched out of his hand. He watched her taken from him again, his eyes filled with horror and rage. The bruised man tied Benji's hands together then took another zip tie from his pocket.

'It's my last one,' he said to the man with the knife.

'Well, use it on the other one,' said knife man angrily, pointing to Colin. Colin's wrists were also bound then the bruised man stepped back, giving way to his burlier colleague.

'Now,' said knife man, 'if anyone's thinking of going anywhere, just remember, you're going to have to get through me, him'—he pointed at the bruised man—'and Nicky over there.' He pointed to the man at the door who also held a large knife. 'I don't know about you,' he continued, 'but I don't fancy your chances much, do you? Now, let's just settle down and have a nice wee chat, shall we?'

***

'Where are they?' said Gemma for the third time. She was crouched in the back of the van with Suzanne, attending to the dogs, who were all being remarkably well behaved considering what they'd been through. In

131

addition to the various facial injuries, one of the fighting dogs had had his ears deliberately cut off. Gemma reckoned, at the very least, Benji would need to get some antiseptic on them. This ear-cutting procedure was performed on dogs by truly stupid, cruel people to make the dogs look more aggressive and be more effective in the pit. No other dog could bite you by the ear if you had no ears. Now, in the confines of the van, having undergone this botched surgery followed by a hurried rescue, it merely served to make the pit bull in question look utterly vulnerable. Gemma stuck her fingers into the carrier, and he licked them gently.

Suzanne filled water bowls and feed bowls, and the dogs lapped at them gratefully. They'd kept the fighting dogs on the opposite side of the van from the bait dogs, just in case, but they all seemed equally as confused, relieved and hungry as each other. The two women had lost track of time while they'd busily attended to the dogs, and as Gemma wondered where the others were for a fourth time, a concerned look swept across Suzanne's face.

'Should I go and check on Carly?' she said.

'Yes,' said Gemma without hesitation. 'Then come back here and tell me what you find.' Suzanne crawled out of the back of the van to investigate. She returned in less than two minutes. Her face was white.

'Carly's not at her post, and I found this.' She held out one of Carly's crutches in front of her.

Gemma cursed and looked into the middle distance, formulating a plan in her head. 'Anything else?' she said.

Suzanne nodded. 'There's a white BMW in the alleyway.'

'Figures,' muttered Gemma. 'Right, here's what we're going to do.'

Benji's heart was thumping hard in his chest while his eyes darted around, trying to see any way out. Their only exit was blocked by a man holding a knife, and he, Colin and Carly were all tied up. Sure, he and Colin could run, but where to? He'd never leave Carly behind though. In fact, he'd give his life to protect her. He glanced over at her. She was looking at the men and all around her. He guessed her thoughts were similar to his.

'So,' said the burly man with the knife, 'let's start with a simple question, shall we? Who the hell are you?'

'We're just here for the dogs,' said Carly.

'Oooh, you're the spokesman are you, sweetheart? Under the thumb, are we lads? Okay, just tell me where the rest of the dogs are, and we'll be on our way.'

'They're not yours,' said Carly.

He raised his eyebrows. 'Feisty one, ain't she, Chaz?' He addressed the man with the bruise, who merely sneered. 'Well, not that it's any of your business, but we're owed these dogs by some associates, by way of payment. They're in debt to us, you see. So, again, where are the dogs?'

'You're not getting them back,' said Carly.

His face transformed from cocky to menacing in a flash. 'Now I'm getting a bit fucking sick of your lip, love, so unless the next words out your mouth are telling me where the fucking dogs are, just shut up, or I'll come over there and ruin that pretty mouth of yours, permanently.' He brandished the knife at Carly.

'Hey!' shouted Benji. Everyone looked at him. He'd even surprised himself by how loudly it had come out.

'She your girlfriend, is she? The spaz?'

Benji could feel his anger rising, the strength of it

making him scared of what he might do. If he rushed forwards and got stabbed that wouldn't do anyone any good, but this guy was pushing him beyond the limit.

'Oohoo, you've made him angry boss,' said Chaz, cackling like a madman. Benji felt his face burn with rising blood, and he ground his teeth together.

'Maybe you could tell us where the dogs are?' said the boss.

'Go to hell,' said Benji.

'Jesus! Can't get a straight answer, can we, Chaz?'

'Nup,' said Chaz. 'How about him?' he said, pointing to Colin.

'Ah yes, you've been awfully quiet at the end there. So, you gonna tell me where the dogs are? They're very valuable to me, you know.'

Colin was silent. Benji glanced past him and noticed the collie was trying to back out of her slip lead, but it kept getting caught on her long fur. Nobody else seemed to have noticed. Benji knew that Border collies were the most intelligent of all the breeds, so if she did get free, he hoped she would be smart enough to avoid these thugs. The boss advanced towards Colin, who was sweating but still silent. Colin glanced over to Bella. The boss noticed and looked too. Bella was straining on her lead to get to Colin, and as Colin returned her pained look, a penny visibly dropped in the mind of the gangster.

'That your dog, is it?' asked the boss.

Colin didn't answer, but his eyes said everything his mouth did not.

'Some nasty men steal it off you, did they?' said the boss, approaching Bella. Colin began to shake slightly, and the sweat dripped down his temples. He looked on the verge of tears.

134

'I've seen a lot of dogs hurt in my time,' said the boss. He crouched beside Bella and looked at her with mock concern. 'They really feel pain, you know? The yelping sound they make when you cut out their microchip, for example, just goes right through you.' He pointed at Bella with the knife, and she came dangerously close to coming in contact with the blade while she jumped and strained towards Colin. The man grabbed her by the scruff, and her whimpering escalated quickly into loud whining and yelps. Her eyes wide with fear, she looked to Colin for help.

'Okay, I'll tell you, just don't hurt her.' Colin was breathing heavily, not daring to look at the others. His eyes were fixed on Bella, the boss and the knife.

'Now then,' said the boss, straightening up, 'that wasn't so hard, was it?' A terrifying grin formed on his face.

There was a sudden scraping noise as Carly shifted in her chair. Benji looked over. She was beginning to spasm. 'Untie her!' shouted Benji. The boss looked over at Chaz and shook his head. Chaz advanced towards Benji with a threatening look on his face. Carly was trying hard to curb the shaking, but she was so stressed that she had no control. Her face went red, and it contorted in a desperate attempt to regain power over her body.

'Untie her!' said Benji again.

'Fuck off,' said Chaz.

'She's got a condition—'

There was a clatter and a thud. Carly's spasms had got so violent that her chair had fallen over with her still tied to it. Benji dodged Chaz and rushed over to her. He crouched down beside her and laid his arms on his shaking wife, wishing his hands weren't tied and he could do more to help her.

'Come on, man,' he said to Chaz. 'Where's she going to go?' He looked over to Nicky by the door. Chaz glanced at the boss.

'Leave her,' said the boss in a warning tone, in case Chaz was thinking of showing an ounce of humanity. 'Now, where were we? Oh yes, you were going to tell me where my dogs are.'

'But you have to let us go first,' said Colin shakily. 'Untie us and let us go, then I'll tell you.'

Benji appraised their situation and felt powerless. Carly was writhing, helpless on the floor, and there was nothing he could do to help her. Colin and the boss man seemed to be about to blow the whole operation, thanks to the anger oozing out of them both. The boss's grin turned to a grimace, and he lunged at Colin with the knife. Colin stumbled backwards, his hands still tied in front of him. The boss lunged again and caught Colin's hand with the tip of the knife. Colin cried out in pain. Just as the boss was about to lunge forwards for a third time, he fell to the ground in agony, dropping his knife. Everyone looked on in surprise to see the Border collie had finally broken free and had decided to sink her teeth into his ankle. Benji seized his opportunity amid the confusion to break free of his zip ties in the way Gemma had taught him. He stood up, raised his arms up in front of him and brought them down with great speed and force across his hips. The ties broke, and he rushed to help Carly.

Chaz was temporarily indecisive. Should he help the boss or stop Benji and Carly from getting free? While he was contemplating his dilemma, the door clanged open with such force that it threw Nicky to the floor, sending his knife flying out of his hand and knocking him out cold when his head hit the concrete. Benji, having undone one of Carly's zip ties, looked up to see Suzanne and Gemma in the doorway.

Seventeen

'Grab that,' said Gemma, and Suzanne immediately seized the dropped knife. Gemma herself was armed with nothing but Carly's other crutch. Benji busied himself untying Carly and protecting her from what was bound to be a fairly violent few minutes. Colin had rushed over to Bella and was protecting her in a similar way.

Gemma kicked at Nicky to check he was out then turned her attention to Chaz. The boss was still being mauled by the collie. Chaz grabbed the boss' knife and squared up to Gemma and Suzanne. It was at this point that Gemma and Chaz looked at each other and said 'You!' in unison.

Gemma couldn't believe her eyes, and it seemed, neither could Chaz. He subconsciously stroked his bruise. He was the guy from the pub whom she'd kicked in the face only days earlier. She'd known he was a bad 'un. He became instantly incensed and ran at her with the knife. She fended him off with the crutch, but he grabbed the end of it and pulled her towards him. His rage was palpable when he raised the knife, ready to drive it into her. She put her stookie up in front of her. The knife hit it and glanced off. Before he was able to recover himself, she took the crutch, placed it between his legs and brought it up sharply. He doubled over in pain. She strode up to him and bashed him hard on the head with the heavy, solid stookie, knocking him out.

Meanwhile, Suzanne had grabbed the collie's empty slip lead. The boss was still thrashing around on the floor, trying to free himself from the collie's vice-like grip. He'd managed to sit up and was trying to hit out at the dog. Suzanne looked unsure. She kicked the knife over towards where Benji was, and he picked it up, Carly still spasming by his side. Suzanne's training session with Gemma came back to her as she stood behind the wriggling boss. She slipped the lead around his neck and began to pull backwards. He made a gagging sound, and she wrestled with him like he was a saltwater crocodile. He alternated between trying to pull the lead away from his neck and swiping at Suzanne. Gemma jogged over.

'Help them,' said Carly to Benji, who was still trying to calm her shaking body. Her hands were now free. He nodded, left the knife with her and approached the only gangster left conscious. The boss grabbed at his throat, still trying to loosen Suzanne's grip, but it was no use, she held firm.

'Hey, Trixie,' said Gemma to the collie. 'Good to see you, girl.' Trixie let go at the sound of her name, and Gemma took the ends of the lead from Suzanne in one hand.

'Take his legs and flip him over,' she said to Benji.

Benji did as he was told. Gemma put her foot on the gangster's back and finally released the lead from his throat. She threw it to Suzanne who grabbed his wrists and tied his hands together behind his back, while Benji held him firmly. Trixie ran around and barked excitedly.

The boss tried to get off his front, but Gemma kicked him in the guts when he turned, and he was semi-immobile again.

'There are more leads in the cupboard there,' said Colin. He seemed reluctant to leave Bella's side but eager to help. Suzanne ran to get them. The boss man tried to struggle to his feet, but it was useless. Suzanne returned with the slip leads, and Gemma instructed her and Benji on how to tie each man up so he would be unable to move.

'It's called the reverse hogtie,' said Gemma, admiring their handy work. 'Don't Google it.' She picked up the temporarily weaponised crutch and returned it to Carly.

All three gangsters were secured and only one was screaming about recriminations through his gag. Gemma patted them all down and took their phones for evidence. Gathering up the bolt cutters, muzzles and leads, Benji, Gemma, Carly, Suzanne, Colin, Bella and Trixie took their leave. They headed straight to the van after securing the door to the building with a new padlock they'd found inside. Benji bound Colin's cut hand and advised him to go to A & E to get it checked out, even though it probably wouldn't need stitches.

'Let's get out of here,' said Benji.

'Agreed,' said Carly, hugging him.

They flopped inside the van with the dogs. Gemma and Suzanne, with Trixie in tow, went to ride up front. Trixie happily followed Gemma, jumping into the cab with ease. She was the epitome of an obedient, friendly dog, despite her soft beautiful fur still being slightly bloodstained. Colin joined them with Bella. The van took off, and they drove through the quiet streets, all the time trying to process what had just happened. As they made their way back to the city, the van blended into the Edinburgh traffic. There was a palpable calming of the atmosphere while everyone's heart rates returned to normal. The partition was open between the front and the back, and Colin was the first to break the silence.

'Wait a minute,' he said, 'what's going to happen to those guys back there?'

'Well,' said Carly, 'they'll be found by the other faction of villains tomorrow, and ... um ... they may destroy each other.'

'Or they may bond over a common enemy,' said Colin.

They all looked towards him, apart from Suzanne who was driving, but even she stole a quick glance. Gemma looked especially thoughtful. 'So, what do you suggest we do?' she said.

'I reckon I call the police when I get home. I want them charged for taking Bella.'

'But they won't get much of a punishment, believe me,' said Gemma. 'Better to let the gangsters sort it out among themselves.'

'Hold on a minute,' said Carly, 'Colin may be on to something. If the cops got hold of the conversations on this phone'—she took Mikey's stolen phone out of her pocket—'those gangsters could get put away, maybe even for a long time. There's loads of evidence against them for a whole range of crimes on here, everything from GBH to extortion. It's all in the WhatsApp groups.'

'Colin could say he found Bella tied up near that building,' said Suzanne, 'along with the phone.'

'I could say I got an anonymous tip-off,' said Colin, warming to his subject, 'so I went out there, discovered

Bella safe and well. The shouts from inside that building were pretty alarming, so I decided to get her to safety before calling the police.'

'There are plenty of links to the puppy farm on the phone,' said Carly, 'maybe we don't need to wait till the other bad guys show up here tomorrow.'

'I could always tell the police they're due to be here tomorrow, so they could set up a sting operation.' Colin was getting quite excited. 'You know, say it was part of the tip-off.'

'I think you're all forgetting something,' said Benji. 'All this would involve lying to the police. Are you sure you're up for that, Colin?'

Colin's excited look faded.

'He's right,' said Gemma. 'It's not even the moral aspect of that. It's more that your story will clash so badly with the bad guys' story that the cops may have trouble building a case.'

They were all quiet for a while as the van trundled its way towards Colin's house.

'Okay, how about this,' said Suzanne, 'what if Colin just tells the truth?'

'You don't understand—' began Gemma.

'Well, not the whole truth, obviously,' qualified Suzanne. There was noticeable relief in the van. She then outlined a plan whereby Colin would tell the police he'd been contacted by a secret organisation online, which he had, met with one of them anonymously, which he had, then agreed to go with them to help rescue Bella, which he had. 'Then,' said Suzanne, 'he could just tell them everything that went on as it happened and say we bundled him into the van with the dogs, dropped him at home, gave him the phone and told him to contact the police.'

'So essentially, he'd just tell the truth, but say to the police he doesn't know anything about us. Bit of a stretch, isn't it?' said Gemma.

'It's true though! Plus, it would make it easier to explain about my hand.' said Colin.

'I could absolutely cover our tracks online,' said Carly. 'The police wouldn't be able to trace our communications with Colin, and if we have any problems, our contact at Police Scotland will help us out.'

'Well, they've never found us before, even though some pretty shady characters have given the cops our description.' Gemma grinned. 'But they're bound to ask what kind of a person you are to meet strangers and go with them in a van to confront sketchy members of an organised crime syndicate.'

'The kind of person,' said Colin, 'who really loves his dog.' He cuddled Bella and buried his face in her fur.

**

They drew up to the park near Colin's house. It was very peaceful. Everyone was at work. They'd agreed to drop him there to be less obvious to the neighbours. Carly handed Colin the phone and got him to swear on pain of death not to lose it. He put it securely in the pocket of his cords.

'You'll be alright?' asked Carly.

'Yes,' said Colin. 'I've got Bella now, and she seems fine, thanks to all of you.'

'And you won't identify any of us?' said Gemma in a warning tone.

'I'll keep the descriptions vague,' said Colin. 'I'm forever grateful, Gemma. I'd never betray you.'

'Right, let's move,' said Gemma, never one for sentimentality.

Carly and Benji snuggled down together in the back, and Gemma set her eyes on the road. Suzanne waved to Colin as they drew away and he waved back. She watched him let Bella off the lead and the two of them chase each other around the deserted park. It was a picture of pure joy. She smiled to herself and drove towards the lock-up.

Eighteen

Gemma was by herself in the lock-up. Well, she was the only human in there. Carly and Benji had headed home for some well-earned rest. Suzanne had helped them return all the stolen dogs, just as they had the night after the dog fight. She was home safely with her parents, doing whatever jewellery sales people who moonlight as animal liberation vigilantes do on a Tuesday night. Gemma lay on her low camp bed and looked at the ceiling. It was finally all over. They had sent the police all the footage and all the evidence they had, and she would send them the phones – all carefully wiped clean – in the morning. The dogs counted as evidence, but Gemma was determined they'd not be treated as such. They'd suffered enough. There were the shaky but clear enough videos from the dreadful puppy farm and dog fight, the photographs of mothers and puppies living in filth at the farm in Fife and, of course, the pictures they'd snapped of the gangsters' car in West Lothian. They'd also taken some close-ups of the various wounds the dogs had suffered. There would be arrests and hopefully convictions for not only animal cruelty but other crimes of which the law took a dimmer view. The police were probably untying the gangsters at this moment.

People would be punished for hurting animals, but

would they be punished enough? Had they made the right decision to call the cops when they did? What did justice look like anyway? Gemma sighed heavily then heard a whining from the other side of the lock-up.

She got up and walked over to where the noise was coming from. The puppies were all asleep, but she knew it wasn't one of them. She smiled at their innocent little faces, eyes closed, their bellies rising and falling in a peacefully rhythmic motion. Walking past them, she got to a large enclosure. It was where one of the male pit bulls they'd rescued had his accommodation. The enclosure was generous, with a large, comfy bed and toys to play and snuggle with, but it was still an enclosure. His muzzle was off, but he pawed at his face in an agitated manner then at the door and whined loudly again.

He was a stray, so there was no owner to return him to. Some of the injured dogs were strays too, but Benji had taken them to stay in the surgery until he could assess their wounds. This one, whom Gemma had secretly named Han Solo, due to the dark patches on his sides that resembled a waistcoat and his solitary status, had no serious physical injuries. She wondered what psychological scars he bore internally. He eyed Gemma suspiciously at first then curiously. She hunkered down, and he licked her fingers through the bars. Doggie prison. They'd had to put him in here for the puppies' sake. As a trained fighting dog, they had no idea how he'd react to puppies darting around. The scum who trained these dogs often used puppies or kittens to bait a new dog.

Gemma hung her head. There were four dogs still missing. They'd searched everywhere they knew of to look, but the missing dogs were nowhere to be found. She hoped they'd been sold back to their owners for the reward money, but in her heart, she knew they were dead. Carly had anonymously suggested to the police that they look for a pit of dead dogs at the puppy farm. They knew those dead puppies had been dumped there, so why not other innocent bodies? She pictured the four dogs in her mind. A chihuahua called Dennis, a pug called Pete, a dachshund called Poppy and a papillon called Mimi. She shuddered. She could call their photos to her mind so easily. They had been pictured with toys, on comfy beds, with adoring owners. She was as sure as she could be that the cats were dead too. Nobody deserved this. Gemma tried to concentrate on breathing deeply and not on their fate, but it was tricky. She knew there would have been other strays, larger dogs, picked up for fighting who would have met their fate on Saturday, possibly after never having been loved at all. She'd been there, within splatter distance of the pit, and she still hadn't been able to stop it. She remembered the lust for blood that had surrounded her and the smell of the place. She touched her broken arm.

Her breathing must have become shallow, because Han Solo was beginning to whine again. He knew she was upset. She raised her head to look at him and almost broke down at the sight of his eyes. They were eyes that said, *What did I do wrong?* He had no idea why he'd been trained to fight. He had probably been abandoned or abused before that then, finally, brought to this place where he was being treated kindly but where he still felt alone. *Screw it,* thought Gemma. She grabbed a muzzle and walked into his enclosure to put it on. He let her do it without any fuss, just seeming happy to be let out. He plodded past the puppies, not giving them a second glance, and walked deliberately towards Gemma's bed.

147

She followed him. She sat on the bed, observing him. He sniffed around the full perimeter of the bed, checking to see if all was safe. He then returned to where Gemma was sitting and sat in front of her. She scratched his ears, and after a short while, he closed his eyes in bliss. She began to feel sleepy herself. The action of the day had taken it out of her, but anxiety and thoughts of dogs lost had kept sleep from coming. She felt relaxed enough to let Han Solo wander about the lock-up. His bed was still available through an open door, and if there were any problems, she'd be woken by barking. He still had his breathable muzzle on.

She lay down on the bed and closed her eyes, one hand still patting the dog by her side. She felt a nudge against her leg and opened her eyes again to see he had one paw up on the bed.

'Oh, you want to come up, do you?' said Gemma, amused.

The bed was a decent size, so she shifted back a bit and patted the space she'd just warmed up. The pit bull didn't need a second invitation. He hopped up, walking round and round in circles before plonking himself down in a tight ball in front of Gemma's stomach. She lay in the foetal position, feeling the warmth of this 'dangerous dog' against her belly. She kept her eyes open for a while, just watching him while he let sleep wash over him at last. He began to snore gently, and his belly rose and fell, just like the puppies' did. As she closed her own eyes and began to drift off, she knew, even though they hadn't managed to save all the dogs, for this dog, at least, life was certainly looking up.

Nineteen

One month later.

'It seems weird that it's their last day here. I've got so used to them,' said Carly, working away at her computer, confirming homes for the French bulldog puppies. They were finally ready to go and had grown quite a bit in the time they'd spent at the lock-up. Carly had set up connections all over the country. Gemma would be taking them down in the van the following day. For now, she sat on the floor beside the little nursery area and pretended to be checking each one over, but really, Carly knew she was having a last cuddle with each of them.

'They all seem to be good,' said Gemma, putting the last one down to go back and play with her litter mates. 'I wonder how they'll do, being separated from each other.'

'I'm sure they'll be fine,' said Carly. 'They're taking more interest in the outside world now than in each other.' It was true. They'd become a massive handful recently ensuring that whoever was sleeping at the lock-up never got much rest.

The group had taken a break from operations since the raid on the gangsters. The bait dogs had been returned to their families and some of the fighting dogs too. There was one dog whose owner was in jail for stabbing a police officer. They'd decided to give his dog to a rehab place that Carly knew just outside of Glasgow. He was now being loved and trained and generally rehabilitated and had been given the name Buddy. The dog who'd had his ears cut off was most probably a stray and was gentle but fearful. Benji had given him a clean bill of health before he'd gone to his new home. He was taken on by a dog trainer Gemma knew who specialised in giving 'damaged' dogs a new lease of life. He was happy and healthy and living with a Rottweiler and three cats. Han Solo was living with an old acquaintance of Gemma's. She'd wanted a special home for him as he seemed so vulnerable, so she'd personally inspected the house in South Queensferry where he was to spend his days. Alex, someone from Gemma's former life, hadn't minded at all, and she and Han had hit it off immediately. He had a big garden to run around in and a loving guardian. Gemma liked the fact that he was within easy visiting distance.

Carly finished her correspondence and was about to go and stretch her legs when her phone pinged.

'News from Tess?' asked Gemma. Their Police Scotland contact could normally be relied upon to give them information that might otherwise be tricky to get hold of.

'There is actually,' said Carly. She had reassured Gemma that the main guys they should be frightened of, the ones they'd tied up, had been arrested not long after all the drama in the abandoned nightclub near Livingston. That had satisfied her, knowing she didn't need to be constantly looking over her shoulder. Well, no more than normal anyway. Carly had more details now, and Gemma was agog. Reading from her phone, Carly recounted the fate of both the Glaswegian gangsters and the Edinburgh puppy farming/dog fighting gang. 'So, apparently Mikey has been given immunity as he's a witness, and he admitted that the phone they have is his.'

Gemma nodded. 'I'm so glad I got it off him,' she said.

'Well, so am I as it seems the phone has proved pretty useful. Mikey's mates, two guys called Stan Price and Greg Sands, have been arrested on charges of theft, animal cruelty, illegal puppy farming and organising an illegal gathering. Obviously, as we know, those offences don't carry much of a punishment, *but*'—Carly paused dramatically—'it turns out they were accessories to some mob activity including kidnapping, extortion and ... eek ... possibly murder.'

'I knew they were scum as soon as they stepped out of that Audi,' said Gemma.

'Yeah.'

'Anyone else going down from the dog fight?'

'Well, it seems that Nobby guy was quite a character, if by character you mean psychopath.'

'The guy whose dog won the fight?' said Gemma. 'Hold on, what do you mean was?'

'It looks like he may have been murdered by the guys we tied up.' Carly went silent for a moment. 'He was involved in all sorts, so I think that's all still under investigation.'

'Oh my God,' said Gemma. 'Maybe it was Stan and Greg's lucky day when they got arrested. You saw their pictures on that restaurant website. They were probably the next intended victims after Nobby.'

There was another silence, while they both processed the seriousness of it all and what might have happened at that abandoned nightclub if they'd left all the villains to sort it out among themselves.

'They're still tracking down and processing blokes from the fight, so hopefully there'll be more convictions there. I'm sure there'll be some that didn't have a criminal record before but will now.'

'So, how are the dogs from the puppy farm getting on?'

'Well, after the dogs were seized and put into the care of the SSPCA ...' Carly scrolled down the information on her phone. 'Loads needed medical attention it says here, no surprises there then.' She thought back to the atmosphere at the puppy farm and felt the familiar feelings of hurt and disgust at how some human beings treated other animals. 'There's no details about the bodies found at the puppy farm, but they did find plenty. I hope they notify the owners if any of the stolen dogs were found.'

Gemma sighed heavily, steadied herself then continued with her questioning. 'And what about Mr Big and the idiot twins?' she said.

'Well, the one they referred to as the boss is apparently known as Freddie "The Ferret" Towser. He is essentially responsible for a quarter of all organised crime in Glasgow and the west.'

Gemma gave a low whistle. 'So, what you're saying is, we've made an enemy of a major gangster. A mob boss no less.'

'Well, yes, but Tess says here that the evidence on the phones could lead to more that would put him away for a long time. I think murder seems to be his main charge, but he's done a bunch of GBH, as you'd imagine, and other things ...' Carly skimmed down the list.

'And we reverse hog-tied him,' said Gemma, beaming maniacally.

'*You* hog-tied him,' corrected Carly.

'It was mainly Suzanne and Benji actually,' said Gemma, grinning and holding her hands up in innocence. Her cast was off, but her arm was still in a brace.

'Well, anyway, it seems that Nicky guy was implicated in a fair bit of this too, so he's still in custody along with the rest of them, but there is some bad news.'

'What's that?' said Gemma.

'Chaz, the one you kicked in the face, is a free man.'

'What?' Gemma stood up, unable to believe her ears.

'According to Tess, he was pretty much just a henchman, and they couldn't find enough evidence to charge him with anything.'

'But the guy's a nutcase,' said Gemma, beginning to pace. 'You just have to look at him to see that.'

'Takes one to know one,' said Carly. Gemma stopped pacing and put her hands on her hips. She gave Carly a long look which Carly returned with mirth. She put her phone back in her pocket and stood up.

'Is that it?' said Gemma.

'For now. It's not a bad result, all things considered. The police are still investigating everyone, so who knows what else they might find. The only thing is the McGregors seem to have got away with everything. Again. They're clearly the owners of the puppy farms and who knows what else, but they just seem to be keeping things at arm's length through their son Mikey.'

'I'd love to take them down,' said Gemma.

'One day.' Carly stretched her back and grabbed her walking stick. 'Pub?' she said.

'Pub.' said Gemma.

Twenty

Waiting for them at the pub were Benji and John. John had been given his puppy pint, a no-alcohol beer especially for dogs, which he was lapping away at contentedly. Suzanne was at the bar, having arrived with Benji, and was getting the drinks in. Carly sat down, and Gemma went to help Suzanne.

'We got some news about the bad guys,' said Carly to Benji. She told him what she'd told Gemma. Just as she was finishing up, Suzanne and Gemma returned with the drinks.

'So, what about the McGregors?' said Benji.

'Well, they just own the place,' said Gemma. 'They're too canny to be caught out. My guess is they had these two guys running things, so if anything went wrong, they'd be out of there pretty quick and not liable for any of it.'

'So, the owners of the puppy farm haven't been arrested?' said Suzanne, looking stricken.

'No, plus Mikey's got immunity for giving evidence, but everyone else was,' said Carly, 'except Gemma's arch-nemesis.'

'The guy I knew from, you know, kicking him in the

face previously,' said Gemma.

There was a silence where everyone tried not to giggle.

'Turns out those guys were some serious gangsters,' said Carly. 'I reckon we should be pretty proud of ourselves for taking most of them off the streets.'

'Yeah, and with all the footage I sent to the police,' said Gemma, 'I'd be surprised if there won't be a few more arrests to come from among those who were at the dog fight. I was careful to get as many faces in the shots as I could. Chances are loads of them will be known to the police anyway. We'll get the McGregors next time.' She sipped her pint and winked at Suzanne, who looked pleased to have been included in the 'next time'.

Gemma scanned the room. She was taken aback to see Jimmy the bartender out drinking with his mates. With more pubs per square mile than anywhere else in Europe, Edinburgh could still be like a small town at times. He wore an unadvisable shirt and chatted easily with the three or four guys who surrounded him. They all looked much like him. He hadn't noticed Gemma. She considered saying hello and then thought better of it. Last time they'd seen each other, she'd left him with an unconscious gangster's henchman to clear up off the floor.

'So, the gang's all here,' said Benji, 'well, apart from Mary.' Mary was with the puppies at the lock-up, to allow them all a chance to get together and debrief.

'And Colin,' said Suzanne. There were general murmurings about Colin's contribution when it came to rescuing the dogs and bringing about these arrests.

'I'd like to propose a toast,' said Carly, holding her gin and tonic aloft. 'To Colin, whom we're so glad was stupid enough to trust a bunch of nutters like us to get his dog back.' She raised her glass, as did the others.

'To Colin!' they said, clinking and sipping.

'Did I hear my name mentioned?' Colin made his way to the table with Bella at his heels, and Suzanne shuffled over to make room for them to sit down. John lumbered over to issue a greeting which Bella met with ladylike civility. Gemma gave Carly a look.

'I just thought I'd let Colin know we were meeting up, so we could share the good news of the arrests and so forth …' Carly tailed off and made a vague hand gesture. She looked guiltily at Gemma.

Colin gave John a pat, and he started chatting to Benji and Suzanne. Gemma got up and plonked herself right next to Carly.

'Why did you tell him where we were?' she said.

'Because I thought it might be nice to meet up,' said Carly.

'What?' said Gemma. 'Nice? Nice to get the gang together who dragged a civilian into a mess of criminals, some of whom are us?' Gemma was speaking with as little mouth movement as possible.

'Look,' said Carly, swirling her gin and tonic around in its glass, 'I think we did a brilliant job, and okay, we got into some scrapes—'

'That's an understatement!' said Gemma, rolling her eyes.

'Perhaps, but I still think if we want to succeed in getting justice for animals, we need more people on the team. The animals need us, Gemma.'

Gemma knew she was being manipulated but didn't say anything because it was Carly. She had only just accepted that Suzanne would be a useful part of the team.

She was young, sure, but she was clever, a good actor and adored animals. She seemed incredibly keen to make a difference, and Gemma had grown to trust her, especially after the dog fighting episode. She was comfortable with Suzanne now. Well, as comfortable as Gemma got with anyone. But Colin? He was in his late forties, didn't seem particularly fit, cracked under pressure and probably wouldn't be particularly impressed by Gemma's methods.

'I don't know,' she said. 'He's not got the right stuff.'

'That's what you said about Suzanne and now look,' said Carly. She gestured over to where Suzanne was chatting animatedly.

'I was wrong about her, but I'm right about him. I can feel it.' said Gemma.

'Okay, we'll see.' It was the same sort of 'we'll see' that a parent would use when they knew they were right, and they both knew it.

Gemma's thoughts rolled around in her head. She knew she was being stubborn. She knew Carly was right, mainly because she normally was. Her thoughts went to the animals and the greater good and her own ego. She looked around the table and saw people who were willing to risk their own safety to help animals who the law didn't protect. She was proud that she'd started it all but had to acknowledge that this team was pretty amazing.

'I'd like to propose another toast,' she said. 'To us. Fighting for what's right against the odds … and to keeping it all … erm … covert.'

She raised her glass then they all followed, clinking them together and repeating, 'To us!' They all smiled, and as she looked around at their faces, she felt a surge of

... what? Pride? Gratitude? Love? 'And I'd just like to say that I think we make an amazing team, for the animals.'

She looked at Carly who beamed at her and said, 'To the Covert Animal Team!'

'The Covert Animal Team!' They all clinked glasses once again, took a drink then fell back easily into conversation.

'Did you just think of that?' said Gemma.

'Yeah,' said Carly.

'Sounds good.' Gemma smiled and put her arm around her friend.

Just then Jimmy and his friends passed by their table on their way out of the pub. He caught Gemma's eye.

'Well,' he said, 'of all the gin joints in all the world, eh Gemma?'

'Alright, Jimmy?' she said with a short nod, extracting her arm from Carly's shoulders, who gave him a little wave. Jimmy visually scanned the table, and Gemma noticed his eyes linger on Suzanne who smiled at him brightly.

'Nice to see you,' said Jimmy, his eyes returning to Gemma. He made his way round to her and whispered, 'Listen, some guys have been at the pub looking for you.'

Gemma gave him a look that made Jimmy's forehead sweat a little. He quickly added, 'I pleaded ignorance, of course'—Gemma's face relaxed—'but I just thought you should know.'

'Cheers,' she said, in a way that ended the conversation.

She nodded at him once more. He and his friends gathered again and made their way out of the door.

'Who was that?' said Suzanne, a bit too quickly.

'Jimmy,' said Gemma. There was a pause as everyone waited for Gemma to elaborate.

'He's a bartender at a pub we sometimes go to,' said Carly, rolling her eyes at Gemma.

'Oh right,' said Suzanne, feigning indifference. 'Which pub?'

Just then the door swung open again, and Jimmy walked back in, his face a little flushed.

'Gemma,' he said, 'there's a homeless guy outside. Him and his dog are getting hassle off a bunch of neds. I tried to step in but ...'

Gemma was out of her seat before anyone could stop her. Suzanne got up to follow her.

'Be careful,' said Carly, with a concerned but resigned air, like a mum dealing with a bunch of constantly unruly teenagers.

Suzanne nodded at Carly and headed out.

Colin looked over at Benji. 'Should I ...?' he said, making a non-committal move to get out of his chair. Benji shook his head. Colin continued, 'Are you going to ...?'

'No,' said Benji, his tone definite.

'Relax, Colin,' said Carly. 'I don't know if you've noticed, but Gemma can take care of herself.'

Colin eased down into his chair again but still looked awkward.

Carly leaned against Benji. 'Yes,' said Benji, his eyes taking on a faraway look, 'you almost feel sorry for the neds.'

The sound of shouting and thumping penetrated the pub through the typically draughty Edinburgh sash windows. Presently, the noises stopped. Gemma popped back in and downed her pint. 'Another?' she said.

'You're driving tomorrow,' said Carly.

'Yeah. That's hours away yet though.'

Suzanne came back in and told them the guy and the dog were alright and the neds had scarpered. 'I'm Suzanne,' she said to Jimmy, who smiled and offered to buy her a drink. They wandered to the bar together and continued to chat good-naturedly.

Gemma eyed them suspiciously. 'So, it's just anyone who can be part of this team now, is it?' she grumbled to no one in particular. She sat down and waited for someone to bring her a drink. John padded over and, having finished his puppy pint and his doggy socialising with Bella, proceeded to press himself up against Gemma. She took his head in her hands and kissed his furry forehead. He smelled of comfort and love. She scratched his ears, and he responded by licking her face until she giggled in spite of herself. *Humans are okay,* thought Gemma, *but animals are awesome.*

Author's Note

Although this book is entirely fictional, it does have elements of truth. For example, puppy farms like the one described exist. Puppies from these places are indeed sold through fake homes. When puppies or older dogs are stolen, it can be for a variety of reasons, but using them as bait dogs, fighting dogs and for breeding is all real. Crime is inextricably linked to all these activities.

If you have any concerns about the issues raised in this book, please contact the following organisations for information.

Lost dogs:
Local Police
Dog Lost UK - www.doglost.co.uk
Dogs Trust - www.dogstrust.org.uk
Local Rescue Centre

Puppy farming:
One Kind - www.onekind.scot
CARIAD hound - www.cariadcampaign.co.uk
SSPCA- www.scottishspca.org
RSPCA- www.rspca.org.uk

Dog fighting:
The League Against Cruel Sports - www.league.org.uk
SSPCA
RSPCA

Dystonia is a real movement disorder. It's an under diagnosed neurological condition. If you think you may have dystonia or would like to find out more about the condition please contact The Dystonia Society at www.dystonia.org.uk

Acknowledgements

Heartfelt thanks go to my parents, Christine and Gordon. Not only were they dedicated beta readers, but they gave me unwavering encouragement through this daunting transition into a new career. They have supported me lovingly throughout my life and I owe them so very much.

I'm very grateful to Sarah Moyes from the charity One Kind who gave me loads of information on the state of puppy farming in Scotland. Also, thanks go to Suanne Heaney and Phillip Bicknell from the League Against Cruel Sports who gave me valuable facts about dog fighting in the UK. On both puppy farming, dog fighting and general animal welfare issues I'm grateful to Laura Moore of the Scottish SPCA for her help. The book is obviously a work of fiction, but I wouldn't have been confident writing it without some basic facts. There are so many organisations and individuals who work so hard every day to try and combat animal abuse it's impossible to list them all here, but I can only say I admire them greatly and try to support them whenever I can.

Thanks to my editor, Kat Harvey (of Athena Copy) who did a wonderful job of straightening out my tangled prose. She did so much to make my first experience with a professional editor not only efficient but also pleasant and not half as intimidating as I thought it would be! Any mistakes that remain are my own.

I'm grateful to Peter and Caroline O'Connor (of Bespoke Book Covers) who did such a wonderful job on the cover. Just the right amount of intrigue...

Thanks to all my friends who've been so enthusiastic throughout the entire process. Special thanks go to Evita, for being a superb beta reader. I very much appreciated her advice. Thanks also to Stuart for not complaining as I stole Evita's time and for being a lifelong friend.

I'd also like to thank my dog Chewie. It was on our slow meanders that I worked out a lot of plot points and he made sure I spent some time away from my desk each day. He also listened patiently as I read the book aloud, sighing only very occasionally. He is (normally) a calming presence and it goes without saying, a very good boy.

Finally, I'd like to thank my husband Gav. Without him there would be no book. He has always had confidence in me, even when I didn't have confidence in myself. He's been a keen beta reader, a generous provider of both tech support and moral support and he also reminded me to drink my tea before it got cold on many occasions. As a writer I often get lost in thought or forget the time. This would be annoying to anyone else, but Gav bears it with a patience I wish I had. His love for animals and nurturing spirit inspire me every day and I feel unbelievably lucky to be spending my life with him.

About the Author

Heather Hamilton has had many occupations, including photographer, tour guide and dog washer. She has studied both creative writing and psychology at the Open University. A peaceful animal rights advocate, she also has particular interests in the child-free life and the representation of disabled people in fiction and elsewhere. She lives in Edinburgh with her husband and her rescue dog, both of whom are just gorgeous. This is her first book.

Follow her on Twitter @WriterHH or go to www.heatherhamilton.uk for news on forthcoming releases.